HIGHLA

AN EROTIC NOVEL

Sequel to the Highland Bound Trilogy

ELIZA KNIGHT

Table of Contents

****

FIRST EDITION
March 2015

Copyright 2015 © Eliza Knight

Cover Design by Kimberly Killion @ The Killion Group, Inc

Published by Knight Media, LLC
PO Box 324
Mount Airy, MD 21771

ISBN-13: 978-1508848332
ISBN-10: 1508848335

****

DEDICATION

For all of my wonderful readers. Every day I write is a joy because of you.

ACKNOWLEDGMENTS

As always, a book cannot be completed without the assistance of many individuals. I would like to thank the following people for their help in making this book a reality: Angie Hillman, Jennifer Bray-Weber, Tara Kingston, Lizzie Walker, Andrea Snider, The Killion Group, my awesome and supportive family, my readers, and last but never least, my amazing street team. Thank you!

MOON MAGIC

By
Eliza Knight

When thunder crashes
And lightning illuminates
Magic comes to pass.

Thistles sway, dancing
Purple petals and green stems
So very lovely.

Rain falls in crystal torrents
Sparkling drops on fingertips
Liquid Sustenance.

Black clouds shield the sun
Blankets the world in darkness
Takes away our sight.

The castle climbs high
Battlements touching the sky
Striking fear below.

Warriors come now
Their weapons shined and sharpened

Prepared for vengeance.

We will survive this
Surge of ruthless cruelty
For we are strong, wise.

Loneliness touches
Us all and can break hearts
Leaving us wretched.

Massaging the soul
Flexing your capacity
To accept love's hold.

Flames burst destroying
Everything in its path
Leaving all tainted.

The evils of men
Devastate the innocent
Leaving destruction.

Do not surrender
To one who strips you, attempts
To watch you bleed dry.

Fear paralyzes
Only those who allow it
Be strong, be steady.

Afraid of being
Broken leaves one hopeless and
The future stark, bleak.

When hope does soar high
So too does joy and pleasure
Fostering courage.

Brave and courageous
Forge ahead leaving the past
And tumbling forward.

Beneath moon magic
Lovers gentle strokes bring bliss
And sweet surrender.

A precious ending
A love that shan't be broken
By the bonds of time.

Eliza Knight

CHAPTER ONE

Inverness, Scotland
1543

"WHAT will ye be having today, master of the sword?" Hildie slipped her hand beneath Ewan's plaid and wrapped her fingers around his waiting cock.

Sir Ewan Fraser — second-in-command to Laird Logan Grant of Castle Gealach — grinned at the willing wench. Aye, the room was not exactly fresh, nor the sheets he lay on, but what more could he expect from a local tavern? He wasn't here for honorable reasons by any stretch of the imagination.

"I'll be having the usual, love—ye and three of your bonny lasses." He wiggled his brows at the tittering females who stood expectantly behind Hildie.

She stuck out her bottom lip in a pout. "For once I didna want to share ye," she muttered, but it was too late, as Ewan had already beckoned the three of them forward.

"Since when do ye not like to share?" he teased, plucking her on the chin. His laird had given him express orders that he visit and enjoy himself at Hildie's establishment on his way back from his duties.

Logan—his laird and closest friend—had sent him out on a scouting mission. Ewan and the dozen Grant warriors traveling with him had not spotted any of the MacDonalds who'd attacked Castle Gealach once more, tormenting the villagers just outside the walls and setting flames to the newly planted fields before running off like cowards.

If the bastards thought they could starve them out or frighten them into handing over their lands, they were even more foolish than Ewan and Logan had thought. They'd been battling the blasted MacDonalds for years now, and it would seem all was for naught, since the animals would never win. Laird MacDonald had tried hard to expose Laird Grant's secrets, and the secrets of the castle, to usurp the Scottish king, even. *God rest his soul*. MacDonald and his clan had ballocks of iron, and one of these days, Ewan and Logan would see those bastards burn.

Ewan was always ready to put his sword to any MacDonald who crossed paths with him. His life had nearly been taken by one of the enemy clan members several months back. A brutal, savage attack it had been when he attempted to protect his laird. He was well enough now to exact his revenge on every damn one of them.

"Why do ye frown so, warrior? Have we not made ye smile?"

Ewan grunted and grinned at the saucy wench.

Hildie climbed up onto the bed and knelt between his thighs, taking his cock into her luscious mouth—causing all thoughts of the MacDonalds to quickly disappear.

A delectable blonde pressed her naked breasts to his face, and another ran her hands over his chest—while yet another knelt beside Hildie to stroke her tongue over his sac. Ewan groaned, licking and suckling at the nipples dangling in his face, while stroking a round arse with each hand. What a life he'd created for himself. As Captain of the Guard, he had more wenches vying for his attention than he could handle. Especially now that his once lascivious laird had married. That left more for Ewan. And he was *more* than happy to take Logan's place.

And Hildie's tongue… Blast, but it felt so good.

"Och, lassies…" he said through gritted teeth. "Ye know how to make a man smile."

Hildie stopped abruptly, motioning for her companion to straddle Ewan, then helped to guide his cock inside. He could hardly suppress a groan as the newest wench slowly slid down the length of his arousal. They were killing him with such sweet, succulent torture.

"I suppose I can share," Hildie murmured, winking at him. *God's teeth.*

The wench was a tease, for certain, but he could barely think with the other one bouncing on top of him. What would he do without these bawdy lassies?

"One of ye straddle my face," he commanded, gripping the randy lass's hips to slow her movements.

Hildie and her two friends giggled, shoving at each other until one of them tickled the other two enough that she won.

"Not every man likes this," she said with an excited grin.

Ewan chuckled. "I love it more than most." He gripped her thighs and guided her until she had a knee on either side of his head, her cunt ready for his tongue. While he fucked one and licked the other, the remaining two lay on the bed beside him and entertained themselves. Och, but this was the life. He knew Logan was happy with his beautiful wife, but did he really know what he was missing? Not that Ewan had any intention of reminding him. He'd be more than happy to service the ladies at Hildie's for years to come.

A crash sounded from below stairs. Two of his lovers cried out in surprise. The lass riding him, didn't seem to notice, she tightened over him, riding him faster and harder. Her sex clenched and spasmed. A moan escaped her lips as stomping sounded on the stairs. His fun was about to be over, no use holding back.

Ewan gripped the thighs of the woman over his mouth and licked her into a climax. A feral growl wrenched from his throat as his own release rippled through him — but the sounds from his mouth were drowned out by the shouts from the corridor just outside the room.

The door opened, but Ewan couldn't see who it was around the wench's thighs.

"Sir, the MacDonalds have been spotted."

"Hell," he growled. Playtime was most definitely over.

Ewan gently tossed his playmates aside. He climbed from the bed to wash his face in the basin then donned his weapons, before tossing a few coins onto the mattress. "I'll return, dinna fash. In the meantime, *amuse* yourselves."

If there was one thing he loved more than fucking women — it was adventure and battle. The rush that fueled his blood when danger was in sight was addictive. Ewan wasn't afraid of dying. In fact, he courted death at every turn. So far, the dark one had shunned him.

He grinned as he jogged down the tavern stairs, the sound of feminine laughs and moans following him. With a mischievous grin and a slight pang that he couldn't join in the festivities he walked out into the sun. Bounding onto his horse, he could already feel his blood burning with the need to swing his sword.

"Onward," he bellowed. "The devil waits for no man!"

Ewan rode swiftly from the tavern, his warriors in his wake.

A shrill whistle pierced the air followed by a bellow that had Shona ducking in fear. All of the herbs she'd gathered in her basket tumbled to the forest floor in a cascade of green and brown.

What in bloody hell was that?

A warning of some type? Tucked back in the woods a safe distance from the village, the only people who could be making such a racket would not be of the innocent type. She glanced around, though the sun was out and bright, with the trees full and green with spring vibrancy, it was hard to see anything. Birds flew out of their perches overhead, disturbed by the sudden interruption of the peaceful wood.

"Idiots," she murmured in regards to whoever was scaring away the wildlife. "How dare they disturb my forest friends?"

Sadly, they were the only friends she had—the birds, squirrels, rabbits, deer and other woodland creatures.

She set down her basket and gathered up her herbs, keeping her eyes wide for any movement—even if it were just a little mouse. The ground rumbled around her and another warning call split the tranquility of the forest.

Devil's toes, but she'd best hide. Though she wasn't completely visible as she foraged in the wood, she was not completely hidden, either. The trees and brambles were thick, but her red hair stuck out like a flag to any who would wish her harm. Though she could probably fight off a single, weak attacker, she'd not be able to get past more than that—and on foot. She had no horse, but even if she did, it had been such a lovely day, she'd been looking forward to a nice walk. The Highlands had gotten nothing but rain the past week. Who knew when the summer storms would pick up again?

Thank the saints she'd not decided to search out daisies in the clearing beyond where she crouched now; else whomever was tromping through her forest would have had a clear view of her.

Shona pulled her *arisaid* over her head to cover her hair, and listened for the sounds of running feet. Panic tried to worm its way inside her, but she held it at bay. There were more important things to concentrate on, such as whether or not she could hear the approach of those in the woods. The earth vibrated beneath her. Standing, she cocked her head to listen. The sounds of men's shouts carried on the wind from somewhere to her right. Not too loud, which meant they weren't as close as she originally thought. To her dismay, there

19

was most assuredly more than one—more like a dozen at least. Not good odds for her.

Closing her eyes she prayed the noise would go away, that perhaps they would take their displeasure elsewhere, but the sounds did not dissipate and they did not fade. If anything, they seemed to grow closer. The birds continued to fly from their perches in the trees, and, overhead, a crow squawked its irritation.

Animals scurried in fear; the noises they made as they trampled over the forest floor only muffled the noise of the intruders. Shona couldn't decipher which was friend and which was foe.

It didn't matter. At this rate, they'd be on top of her before she had a chance to escape them if she didn't get moving. The road through the forest was a brisk three-minute walk from where she stood, and no trouble had come to it in months. This far into the forest, she rarely encountered anyone. 'Twas the reason her Rory had chosen it.

Though, she supposed after what had happened to Rory, she should have been more wary.

Shona turned to count the number of arrows in her quiver—six. She was a good shot. Rory had seen to it. But six wasn't nearly enough arrows to take out the number of warriors she was certain she heard.

Lord how she missed Rory. He'd sheltered her for years. And then one day—he'd simply disappeared. She feared him dead, for it had been at least two years now since he'd left to purchase a mule and not returned.

The sounds of the disgruntled men grew closer still, and her hands started to shake. She held tight to her basket, not wanting to drop it and give them any reason to come searching for her. Living alone in her isolated cottage, trouble was the last thing she needed.

"Nettles," she grumbled her preference mild expletive.

She tucked her basket into the crook of her elbow, and gathered up her skirts in her hands so the hem didn't tangle with her feet.

If her errand had to be cut short, at least she wouldn't go home empty-handed. She needed these herbs for the latest tincture she was working on. Despite her home being isolated, there were a few who knew of her existence—namely the healers from the surrounding villages. They often came to her for her powders, tinctures and ointments. Shona had a gift that no one seemed able to duplicate.

She stilled her walking to listen to the sounds of the forest. At least for now, the intruders were still a safe distance away. Well, not *exactly* safe. She slipped into a narrow passage of rocks that lead down a hill, using the natural cover to check for any scouts hiding up or behind any of the trees. She saw nothing, but the shouting seemed to grow louder with every passing second.

She sent up a prayer that she crossed no one. Though deep in the wood *she* rarely came across anyone, Castle Gealach, and Scotland itself, often had unfriendly visitors. Most of them raiders or rival clans trying to pillage and destroy. Shona wanted no part of that.

Not too far from the road now. She slipped from the rocks and continued. She stepped over fallen branches making sure to land softly on patches of moss and grass that would make little or no sound.

The scents of the forest and the herbs in her basket normally calmed her, and on most days, she enjoyed being alone. She liked working with plants. She liked knowing that she could help someone, even if they never met. But she did miss Rory. His company had been sweet, he'd taught her many things, and he'd been her protector since she first arrived in the area. There were some days when the cottage and surrounding wood seemed too quiet.

Now he was gone. Whether he'd left her, befallen some awful accident, or met a foe upon the road, she had no idea—a fact that pained her immeasurably. She'd searched the forest for days, weeks, months on end with no sign. 'Twas as if he'd disappeared into thin air.

She knew little of his past and nothing of any family he might have had, and so she could not contact them to find out if he were there, or to inform them she believed something had happened. Rory had not wished to speak of his family. Which served her fine. She did not remember her own.

Shona stepped lightly through the forest, pausing beside trees every few feet to check for sounds. Angry shouts and horses whinnying sent a shiver over her spine. They were close — or possibly she'd been walking right toward them, so deep in thought had she been.

Silencing a frustrated groan that itched to leave her throat, she studied her surroundings, spying the road up ahead. Her entire body trembled. She was extremely anxious to get home. To get away from whoever was marching through the forest.

She had to get home. Had to.

Not that there would be anyone to answer to. With Rory gone and no family to turn to, she'd been forced to remain alone these past two years. She'd made a good go of it so far. And having the freedom of answering only to herself was kind of nice. Though loneliness often crept in, she was good at pushing it away. Mayhap she could have begged the help of Laird Grant and his lady wife at Castle Gealach, but... Shona wasn't one to beg. She didn't want to serve anyone within the castle, nor be beholden to a master.

She'd have to fend for herself. Most of the time. Rory had taught her a lot since they'd met. He was an outcast warrior from a neighboring clan, waiting out the days until he could approach Laird Grant about joining his clan army. But that day had never come.

Shona shivered and shook her head. Nay, she could not go to the castle. Ever.

A bellow, so close it could have been beside her, startled Shona. She dropped to the ground in a crouch, her heart pounding out of her chest, a whimper on her lips.

More roars ensued, followed by metal clanging and the thunder of a many hooves.

God's teeth, they sounded as though they were practically on top of her. She waited for the sharp pain of the horse's hooves crashing over her head.

CHAPTER TWO

WHERE in bloody hell were they?

Ewan gripped the reins of his horse, Bhaltair, and turned him in a circle. A dozen warriors rode with him through the wood, trying to ferret out the MacDonalds. *Traitorous bastards.* He'd counted at least nine of them getting away.

Though he'd seen four McDonalds on horseback, the rest were on foot, and they couldn't have outrun Ewan. They were hiding. Laying low.

Well, not for long.

"Come on out and face us like men, ye limp-cocks!" Ewan shouted, raising his sword in the air, gaining a few laughs from his men.

The MacDonalds had been pulling these raids for a week now, and while Ewan and his men had picked off the few who'd straggled behind, the rest of them had taken flight.

A fact that only enflamed his anger. For the MacDonalds to have been able to storm onto the lands so efficiently — they had to be hiding somewhere in the woods. But he and his men had scoured the area and found nothing — both over the past few days and just now when the bastards had been spotted.

Ewan hated to admit that the MacDonalds might have the upper hand. Nay, he refused to believe it. For as long as they'd been trying, the bloody jackanapes had not been able to win more than a mere skirmish. The Grants had outfought them in all other regards. They'd not been able to succeed in capturing Castle Gealach, nor any part of the lands each and every time they'd tried. But they had succeeded in terrorizing the people and getting away. The few they'd been able to capture were close-mouthed about their comrades — and currently knocked out cold and tied to a tree with three guards standing watch.

"Will ye make us wait all day for a fight, ye cowards?" Ewan cried out once more.

There was no answering call, but to his right he thought he heard something scurrying around. Ewan swung Bhaltair to the right and pointed his sword into the trees.

"I can hear ye. Ye'll not be able to hide from me for long. Your arse is mine!"

Ewan nodded to his warriors and spun his sword in the air, pointing for half of them to go one way and the other half to go another. They'd close in on their enemies soon.

"Captain, should ye be going alone?" his lieutenant, Lachlan, questioned.

Ewan frowned at the man. By his count there was less than a dozen MacDonalds left from the raid. He could easily take on four at a time. "I'm not alone. The lot of ye lads will be within yards of me."

Lachlan nodded. "Aye, Captain, but they've got the Butcher with them."

The Butcher.

Ewan had heard of the devil. A man so brutal, so cruel, that his own mother had tossed him from a cliff after he was born. Legend stated that he'd taken his tiny bairn fists, climbed back to the top of the ledge and pushed his mother off. In the past week, the man had left his signature on several of the Grant crofters — men, women and children. His name alone made Ewan hot with rage.

"The Butcher will pay for what he's done to our people." Ewan flicked his gaze at the men.

They looked as angry as he felt. "Lachlan, ye lead the men around to the right. Gregor, ye take the men around to the left. Flynn, ye're with me."

"Aye, sir," the men murmured, then followed their leaders in formation off of the road and into the trees.

Ewan nodded to Flynn, and the two of them urged their mounts straight ahead into the woods. Their horses were trained to walk silently, so the warriors could listen for sounds that were out of place. One of the clumsy MacDonald fools was bound to let their whereabouts be known.

Out of nowhere, an arrow sailed through the air. The spinning tip swooshed past Ewan's face and landed with a sickening *thunk* in Flynn's shoulder. The force of the blow knocked Flynn from his horse.

Ballocks! The enemy warriors must be in the trees!

Ewan bellowed a war cry, sword drawn. He turned his mount in a circle, prepared to fend off more arrows with his targe. When no one came into view, when no more arrows soared, he dismounted and dragged the bleeding, cursing Flynn to a tree.

"Can ye stand on your own?" Ewan asked.

Flynn nodded. Bracing himself against the tree and using his legs for power, he slid upward, keeping his back against the bark for balance. His face was pale, eyes filled with pain and rage.

"This is going to hurt." Ewan grabbed the shaft of the arrow at his shoulder, not necessarily a deadly wound, but one that bled and hurt like the devil. "Hold tight to the base."

Ewan placed Flynn's fist at the base of the arrow shaft, then gripped the center with his own two hands. He snapped the arrow in half. Flynn growled, his skin growing white as a sheet. They had to leave the arrow where it was until a healer could cauterize the wound or sew him up, but at least having the end of it snapped off would make maneuvering easier.

"Dinna pass out." Ewan retrieved Flynn's sword and set it in the warrior's hand.

"Stay strong, lad. They'll be back."

Ewan stood in front of Flynn and shouted at the trees. "Show yourselves!"

The leaves in the trees rustled, but there was no wind. A moment later, two warriors dropped to the ground, their faces split into evil sneers.

THEY were fighting! Right near her.

Suppressing a shriek, Shona clamped her mouth shut and scurried on her knees toward the wild berry shrubs. Parting the thick branches, she dove through, yanking on her skirts that got caught on a few thorns. Panic tore through her. She shoved her basket, her bow and quiver full of arrows deep into the brush. Then she yanked her dagger from her belt to cut at the branches that held her captive.

She managed to free the fabric in the nick of time, for not a breath later, several of the fighting men broke through the trees and into view. Shona scrunched herself up into the smallest little ball she could, praying none of them stared at the brambles too closely, else they catch sight of her.

Eyes wide, she couldn't still the beating of her heart. She breathed in shallow, quick gasps.

From what she could see, it looked like two men chased another from somewhere near the road toward where she sat. Thank goodness they'd been loud enough to warn her from going that far, else she'd probably be right in the thick of their fighting, if not dead already.

The men tossed crude words at each other.

Shona wanted to squeeze her eyes closed, to cover her ears, but she forced herself to watch and listen. They did not wear the same tartan colors. Rival clans. She could tell that the largest of the three men was from Clan Grant of Castle Gealach. The others looked to be wearing the MacDonald tartan—she'd seen it enough over the years to recognize it as they'd slinked past wherever she was foraging. She also knew that all these men were extremely dangerous. Besides that, Rory had warned her to stay away from the laird's guards. They were dangerous. They would hurt her, take advantage of her. Use her savagely. They would set flames to her house.

They'd call her a witch and condemn her to death by hanging—or worse, they'd drown or burn her. Maybe all three.

She could almost feel the water filling her lungs, the rope tight about her throat, the flames licking up over her feet to her calves, singeing her skin before reaching her knees and thighs. The fabric of her gown would melt away to ash, and her skin with it. Death would not be swift, but a painful descent into darkness.

As she watched them circle each other it was hard not to notice how fine the largest of the lads looked—the one from Clan Grant. He lunged at his opponents, a blur of a beautiful man with golden hair and bronzed skin.

The MacDonald warriors were fearsome and rough. Grit covered their skin and hair. Misshapen facial structures showed what a cruel and hard life they embraced. The vicious snarls coming from them had her stomach turning in knots. She bit down hard on her lip to keep from whimpering, and when she tasted blood brought her knuckles to her lips to bite down upon instead.

The handsome warrior fought hard, pushing his enemies back. But the MacDonald warriors weren't about to be shoved to the ground. One slipped a *sgian dubh* from his sock and swiped haphazardly at the Grant warrior, while the other snuck up from behind.

The larger, golden man jumped back out of the way, but the blade caught on his shirt, ripping a gaping hole, and when he leapt backward, the other took a swipe. The golden one dropped and rolled in an elegant move. She cringed, expecting to see blood on his back. Her stomach dropped to her toes. When no blood came, she let herself breathe out a tiny sigh. The MacDonald idiot must have missed his target.

Though the MacDonald warriors fought viciously, they were no match for the golden god. They lacked a finesse that the warrior held. When one of them finally realized this, he beckoned to his companion, turned his back and ran, shouting for more of his comrades. The other MacDonald hesitated.

Were there more of them? Shona sank further into the bushes, one of the thorns painfully scratching her cheek.

"Cowards," the Grant warrior growled as the second man decided to make a run for it. With a roll of his eyes, the golden one hurled his dagger, catching the other man in the back. He fell to the ground, groaning.

Shona cringed. The dagger protruded from the man's shoulder, blood staining the fabric of his shirt. Either the Grant warrior had no aim, or he'd purposefully targeted the man in a place that would not kill him.

The golden warrior sheathed his claymore and charged toward the writhing man with anger burning in his eyes and a snarl on his lips. Handsome, powerful, fierce. A chill rushed over her. Who was he? When would he leave so she could get back to her cottage before they found her?

And, god's blood, but if he did find her, what would he do? Bile rose in her throat, spurred by fear.

The Grant warrior stuck his boot under the man's belly and flipped him over. He bent low, anger coming off him in waves as he stared down his enemy. "Who sent ye?" he demanded.

But the howling man didn't respond, only rolled back onto his belly, and reached frantically behind him to get the blade. His fingers slipped in his own blood.

The golden warrior, with a huff of annoyance, yanked the blade out, followed by the weaker man's wail of pain. The larger warrior rolled the injured one over, and again said, "Who sent ye?"

The injured man had the nerve to spit in the warrior's face. Shona recoiled. Though the golden warrior had stabbed him—he'd also pulled the blade out.

The Grant warrior shoved his boot against the man's chest, crushing him into the ground.

The ground continued to rumble, and two more men, looking just as desperate and unrefined as the felled one, broke through the trees. By the way the large one reacted, jumping to his feet and drawing his sword once more, he didn't know them. More MacDonalds, judging by the tartans they wore.

Was the forest filled with them?

Shona's stomach was so twisted up in knots she had to keep herself from vomiting. Her throat burned and her head pounded. She was working herself up so much that she'd be sick very soon if she didn't get ahold of herself. At that realization, she forced herself to calm. Aye, she was alone. Aye, all she had was her little dagger and a few arrows for protection. But she was hidden away enough that no one had noticed her yet, and the business they were going about, they'd not notice her at all. That was, if she kept quiet.

She breathed in deeply through her nose, letting it out in a long quiet exhale. *Get a hold of yourself, Shona!* Rory would be rolling in his grave now if he knew how she was responding to these brutes. He'd taught her better than this.

The stark truth was, her life depended on her silence.

Shona clutched her blade all the tighter, ignoring the sting of the handle biting into the flesh of her palm.

The golden warrior turned in a circle, assessing his surroundings. His face remained calm as he looked about, but the steady jerk in his jaw muscle told her that he was a little more concerned than he showed. He glanced behind him, looking relieved. That was odd. 'Twas almost as though he was glad none of his comrades had come forward—if he had comrades at all?

The warrior appeared to be alone, at least that was what he wanted his enemies to think. No one chased after the MacDonald men to come to the Grant warrior's aid. Why had he been on the road alone? Especially with the lands crawling with raiders. As a Grant warrior, he had to have known the risks of doing so.

She'd known them.

'Haps he'd had companions and the MacDonalds had defeated them.

Fear was beginning to take control of her body. Her teeth chattered and she bit down hard enough to make her jaw muscles hurt.

The new arrivals reined in their horses and smiled down on the lone warrior like ghouls. That only seemed to make the Grant Highlander more assured. Puzzling. He grinned up at the two on horseback as though he'd eat them alive within the count of ten.

Cocky warrior, he was.

"We've a message for your laird," one called down with a sneer on his ugly face.

The golden god stared defiantly up at them, his weapon steady, perhaps expecting them to pounce. From his stance, Shona wondered if the message would be this man's death, and she wished she could help him. How, she had no clue, but she couldn't just let him die. Nettles, what was she thinking? She had to remain silent — or die. She owed this warrior nothing. She had to save herself.

But... that just seemed so wrong. Something about the golden one struck her in a place deep inside her chest that moved her to action. Still, she hesitated.

Rory had taught her to throw a knife, but she only had one and she didn't want to hurl it and chance missing — nor did she want to give up the only weapon she could use in case someone pounced on her from behind. She did have her bow and arrows though. Perhaps that was the way to go, though it would take time to notch her arrows — and she'd need to leave the safety of her hiding place.

With that thought, she whipped her head to the side to make certain that no one was sneaking up from the other side. The forest was quiet, save for the three on her right.

"Come and give me the message, then," the golden warrior growled with a twirl of his sword.

The two on horseback circled the warrior, taunting him. Shona had to do something. This warrior was alone, and she couldn't stomach watching him die. There was something about his eyes, something that compelled her to help him. Told her that he was a good man. She muttered a curse. Why was she so torn? She didn't know. She should simply take care of herself and not worry over this man she didn't know. Why should she risk her own neck for a stranger?

But as the two MacDonalds on horseback took swipes at the warrior on foot, she no longer listened to reason. He was bleeding from several wounds—though he'd been able to draw their blood as well. It wasn't a fair fight with them on horseback. The two MacDonalds closed in, each stabbing their swords toward the golden warrior. In her heart, she knew she couldn't sit back. Not when she was able to help. Her conscience wouldn't allow it. She'd live out the rest of her days with his blood on her hands.

Shona blew out a deep breath. There was no more time to waste.

She glanced behind her and saw no one. Quietly backing away from the brush, she edged toward a tree twenty feet to the side of the fight. The men were so involved with their heinous battle that none of them noticed her. Shona nocked her bow with two arrows as Rory had showed her, and took aim. The feathers tickled her cheek. She blew out a deep, slow breath, forcing herself to block out the noise of the forest and the hateful words being tossed back and forth in front of her.

Her heart pounded so hard in her ears, she prayed the men couldn't hear it. Prayed she met her mark, for if she missed, she would be the men's next target. A last draw for breath, she let it out slow once more, closed her eyes, envisioned the men, adjusted her aim, and let the arrows fly.

They whizzed through the forest. Judging by a loud scream, she'd hit at least one of her targets. Shona opened her eyes in time to see the golden warrior react. He leapt up into the air and grabbed hold of the one man who'd not been hit, hauled him to the ground and shoved his sword deep into the man's chest.

Still atop his horse, Shona's arrow protruding from his chest, the second stubborn enemy warrior gripped tight to his reins. In a last act before he succumbed to his wound, he meant to trample her warrior.

Her warrior?

Shona shook her head. She didn't have time to contemplate such imaginings. She nocked another arrow and let it fly. The sharpened tip burrowed into the man just as he yanked back on his reins. The horse reared back on its hind legs, forelegs pawing at the air. So damn close to the warrior's head.

"Look out!" she warned, but it was too late.

As the warrior looked toward where she stood, attempting to dive out of the way, the horse came down on him.

The golden warrior crumpled to the ground, unmoving.

The warhorse then bolted through the trees — his master hanging limply over the side, hopefully dead.

A scream stayed silent on her lips — the enemy had killed her warrior.

CHAPTER THREE

EWAN couldn't move.

He couldn't see, either.

His head pounded with pain, radiating down his spine. The only good part was that the injuries he'd sustained from those bastards on horseback didn't hurt as much.

Was he blinking? He felt like he was blinking, but he couldn't be certain. Everything remained black. He couldn't tell whether his eyes were open or not. He willed himself to keep them closed, just in case, and remained very still, hoping the bastard on horseback had thought him dead and left. Good thing he'd had the forethought to draw the MacDonalds away from

Flynn, he only hoped the lad had been able to escape or find the other Grant warriors.

Wait!

His mind fastened upon one startling question—who was the woman?

She'd shouted a warning to him. Had she been the one to shoot the arrows?

He strained to listen, but the sound of rushing water was pronounced inside his skull. If he'd not felt the ground beneath him, he might have thought he was lying in a loch or the sea, waves crashing over him.

"Oh my god," someone whispered nearby.

'Twas *her*. He was almost certain of it. There was a swishing noise and then a whoosh of air beside him.

"What have I done?" he heard her say.

Ewan tried to shake his head, but any subtle movement pained him, and he wasn't even certain he was moving to begin with.

Who was she with? Was she part of the MacDonald gang? What was she so worried over?

He couldn't remember what she looked like. But he was almost certain he'd never seen her before. She wasn't from Gealach, so she could be a MacDonald. Though there was every possibility she was a fairy, too.

The pull of agony and the rushing water in his head drowned out his thoughts. And then the pain receded to a tingling numbness. He was falling deep inside himself.

And everything was…

SHONA hesitated, breathless with fear.

'Twas her fault the warrior had been hurt. With a darting glance from left to right, and seeing no one, she ran to the warrior's side. He was even more stunning in person. Golden hair with brows that slashed in arches on his broad forehead. Angled bone structure and a strong, chiseled jaw. He was no stranger to fighting, that was apparent. His nose bore a distinct notch where it had been broken several times. Instead of tending to him, she found herself staring at his mouth. A wide mouth with full lips that made her dream of cold winter nights when those lips could be used to warm her. What in Hades was wrong with her?

Shona shivered, feeling shame. This poor man was crumpled on the ground, broken, discarded and she was thinking about kissing. *Him*. She tore her gaze from his lips to stare at his closed eyes.

Without hesitation, Shona pressed her hand to his stubbled cheek, feeling the bristles scrape and tickle over her palm. His skin was warm, and when she held her thumb beneath his nose she felt his breath.

He lives.

Blood soaked his shredded shirt. She needed to find out how many wounds he had sustained beyond the injury to his head. And fast. Though he survived for now, there was still a chance he could die considering the amount of blood seeping from his wounds.

But how could she get him away from here? He wasn't going to walk, and she wouldn't be able to carry him. A few feet away, the warrior's mount bobbed his head, as if nodding that he could help. When had he arrived?

Shona did not know much about warhorses, but she'd heard they held a great bond with their masters. 'Haps the animal had heard his master fall and made certain to come and find him.

The hair on the back of her neck prickled. She didn't know if it was nerves or that she was being watched, but instinct bade her to be careful and quick. Shona checked to make certain there were no other warriors lying in wait. The only thing that appeared to accompany the three of them was a slight breeze that rustled the trees. She stared up at the limbs as they swayed, the branches hiding then revealing the blue, cloudless sky.

Fortunately the weather was agreeable. She couldn't imagine trying to heft this mountain of a man in the slippery mud.

Holding out her hand to the animal, she blew a low whistle. The horse eyed her with suspicion, his head down, ears flicking back and forth. She clucked her tongue, appearing to pique the animal's interest all the more. The horse walked steadily forward, eyeing her with caution.

"'Tis all right," she crooned, making certain to keep her hand out and the rest of herself still. She wanted the animal to know she wasn't a threat. Last thing she needed was to be trampled, too.

The warrior did not move nor did he make a sound—and thank goodness for that else the man might unconsciously spook his horse.

The horse came closer and nudged her palm, lipping her until he realized she was without a treat. With a disgusted snort, he turned his attention to his master. The warhorse lowered his head and with his muzzle, nudged the warrior in the shoulder. The man groaned, but did not stir.

Before the horse could retreat, Shona slid her hands over his neck and mane then wrapped the reins around her wrist. She had hold of the warrior's horse. But what was she going to do? Bring them back to her cottage? That would be dangerous for many reasons. One, the warrior would know where she lived. Two, if anyone was watching them they could follow her home. She really needed a plan. But there was no time to think. What was she going to do?

Shona frowned. How was she supposed to even get him on the horse?

She stared down at his bleeding body. Though it was a gamble, by the look of things, taking him home where all her healing supplies were was the only chance he'd have at living. If she didn't get him back there soon and begin treatment, he would slowly bleed to death.

No matter the risk, she couldn't let that happen.

Once he was well, she could easily drug him with a potion and take him back into the woods and leave him — that was, if no one found them first.

With that semi-solid plan in place, her thoughts were drawn back to the warrior, and how exactly she'd be able to get him onto the horse. What good was having a noble steed if said steed couldn't pick a man up? The warrior was huge. Easily a foot and a half taller than her and likely weighed nearly twice as much. His muscular thigh alone was as thick as her torso.

As if reading her thoughts once more, the horse dipped down onto its forelegs and softly neighed. Shona stared at the magnificent animal, speechless. She'd not had much interaction with warhorses other than Rory's mount. He'd trained him to do a fair many tricks, but not this. How did the animal know he was needed to carry his master?

Forcing herself to recover her surprise, she tucked her hands beneath the warrior. Her fingers met damp warmth — sweat and blood, no doubt. She heaved, not moving him one inch. Lord, but he was heavy. Muscles the weight of iron. She heaved again, digging her feet into the ground and bending her legs. She dragged him about six inches before stopping to take a break. Then she braced herself again and put all her strength into moving him toward the horse.

Somehow, with a lot of grunting, Shona managed to get the warrior's back up against his mount, his head resting on the saddle. Standing, she straightened her back, trying to catch her breath. Her limbs screamed from the exertion, for he was solid sinew. She'd never seen a man so brawny in her life. Not even Rory had been so full of muscle.

Shona blew out a sigh. She had to finish this. The longer she tarried the more likely they were to be in danger. Shoving hard, she rolled him onto his belly, then came over to the other side of the horse and adjusted his arms, so they lay over the side of the saddle.

The man groaned, a sound so woefully pain-filled, tears welled in her eyes.

"I'm sorry to cause ye even more pain, sir," she said. "But if I dinna get ye out of here, ye'll die."

Standing on the opposite side of the lowered horse, she gripped beneath his armpits again and yanked as hard as she could, bracing her feet and using all of her slight weight to help her.

At last, the warrior was draped over the horse. Feeling his master's weight, the horse stood and nudged her elbow.

Shona took hold of the reins and led the horse back to the brambles where her herb basket still lay hidden. How fortunate for the warrior that she'd gathered comfrey and wolfsbane, and that she still had a good supply of garlic, lady's mantle and bog moss at her cottage.

Careful of her surroundings, and listening for any sounds out of the ordinary, she led her two charges back to the road. The dirt-packed path had dozens of divots left by horses for as far as she could see in either direction. Because she wasn't sure how new or old the prints were, or in which direction they'd gone, Shona decided it would be best to keep off the road, even if it meant that it would take longer to get to her cottage.

"Stay strong, lad." She smiled at her boyish reference to the warrior. He was no lad. The strength and imposing bulk of his body made it obvious he was a grown man.

He grunted in reply, shifting enough that she stopped the horse quickly to lay her hand on his arm.

"Dinna move unless ye want to fall and break a leg or arm, ye fool. Stay still and I'll have ye off the horse soon enough."

Shona rolled her eyes. The man's actions were not unlike Rory's would have been. Warriors were used to making decisions in battle, and with the extent of his injuries she was certain he would think he was *still* in battle, rather than atop his horse. He'd be fighting to get away from whoever was taking him, probably not recognizing that he was on his own horse, only that he'd not been the one to make the decision to be there. He might think her an enemy, too. She had to reassure him, else he endanger himself — and her — in the process of trying to escape.

"Ye're safe. I'm a healer," she said. "Now, be still."

Seeming to understand her—or possibly because his injuries had brought sleep to him once more—he stilled.

Her heart pounded as she peered up and down the road. Nothing stood out—other than the hoof prints.

Shona moved across the road and into the woods on the other side. As they navigated quietly through the forest, the sun overhead slowly sank to the horizon so that by the time her small cottage came into view, the sky was grayish pink.

Circling around the woods that surrounded her home, she checked to make sure that no one sat in wait to ambush them. She checked her traps for signs of tampering, and when all looked clear, she led the horse and his master to the front door.

She walked them straight into the main room, praying the horse did not soil her clean floor. Letting the reins drop, she shut and barred the door. Darkness enveloped her. There were two small windows high off the ground, but no light came through the closed shutters.

The horse snorted.

"Just a minute, horse," she said, shuffling toward her small hearth. She found her flint and lit a candle, illuminating her tiny but cozy cottage in golden light.

Her small bed was pushed into the left corner, a chest at the foot of it, and a small wooden table beside it. Adjacent to the door was the empty hearth, and before it sat a table and two chairs. Alongside the hearth, shelves were filled with her medicinal herbs, tinctures and powders. On her right was a modest cupboard, a high table for food preparation, and a wardrobe filled with miscellaneous supplies. Her home was simple and comfortable.

Grabbing the reins once more, she led the animal toward her bed, hoping it would be easier to roll the warrior off the steed onto her mattress than to drag him across the floor. "There now, let him down."

When the horse simply stared at her, she tried another command and nudged him on his withers. "Let him off?"

Again the animal simply stared at her.

Shona let out a frustrated groan. "I need him on the bed, horse, else I canna help him.

The warrior shifted, tapping the horse with his foot. "*Sios...*" His whispered Gaelic — *down* — had been barely audible.

She watched in amazement as the horse once again lowered himself enough that she could roll the warrior onto her bed. He landed with a loud, awkward thump.

"Oh, saints," she hissed with fright.

With quick movements, Shona arranged his legs, frowning at his feet hanging off the edge, but what was she to do? He was enormous. Gently, she put his head on her pillow, and used the linens beneath him to help tug him into the center of the bed. The man managed to move enough to help her, though the painful grunts made her heart skip a beat. By the time she had him situated in the center of her small bed, her hands and sleeves were covered in streaks of his blood.

A shiver of fear filled her and she sent up a prayer that none of his enemies — nor his people — came to find him. Her life depended on it.

How could men do this to one another? She stared hard at her hands, flashes of the fight that had brought about all that blood running rampant in her mind. But she could not dwell on the whys and why nots. She had to take care of this man before he succumbed to his injuries.

His gasps grew short and rattled. Not a good sign.

"Stay with me a little while longer," she whispered.

CHAPTER FOUR

RETURNING her attention to her charge, she studied him with an expert eye. He took up nearly the whole of her bed, feet dangling over the edge. As of that moment, he appeared to be sleeping peacefully — despite his labored breathing.

"I pray ye do not wake up," she whispered.

Cleaning and sewing his wounds would be much easier if he lay there unmoving. Without anyone to assist her, if he woke and thrashed about he could hurt himself — and possibly her, as well.

Where to start? She tugged her knife from her belt and slid the blade from the bottom of his tattered shirt to the top. Tossing the bloodied mess beside her hearth, she then set about examining his wounds. There was a massive knot on his head where the horse's hoof had clobbered him, and a cut about two inches long, though it did not appear very deep. The wound would give him a wicked headache. He'd need a stitch or two there. She moved her gaze to his sculpted torso, which beneath the current wounds and blood, was riddled with scars. What had happened to this man? If she'd not seen him fight, she might have thought him without skill, but that was far from the truth. He was definitely proficient in the art of combat. She'd seen those talents with her very own eyes. But someone had truly gotten the better of him.

A nudge at her elbow had her jerking until she recalled his warhorse. Shona needed to get the animal out of her cottage before he made a mess, but that would have to wait.

She traced over the slices and jabs on the warrior's chest, ribs and belly, her fingers trembling, and her teeth firmly planted in her lower lip. She was surprised to find they were not as extensive as she first imagined. No obvious signs of broken bones, though his ribs would likely be bruised. Even with his significant blood loss, his wounds did not appear to be near any vital organs. And the few direct stab wounds did not appear overly deep. He was lucky. If she could get him cleaned up, stitched and keep any fever at bay, then he'd likely come through this very easily.

After lighting her hearth, she put a kettle of water on to boil, and then began smashing her herbs with oil to make a paste to rub into the wounds. Once the water had boiled, she dipped a cloth into it and wiped away the blood and dirt on the man's torso. She rolled him onto his back and cleaned there, too, trying not to stare too hard at the coiled muscles—or the crisscrossing scars that covered his body.

The scars, while fully healed, were still pink in places. He'd not had them long. He certainly had the worst kind of luck. Nearly butchered, perhaps six months before if she had to wager a guess, and then trampled by a horse today.

Nevertheless, she supposed it was a warrior's life. Rory had scars on his body, too, though not as extensive as these. She vaguely recalled the castle's healer coming to her some months past begging for a salve and tincture to save a man who was near death because of a vengeful wench. Was it possible that the salves and tinctures had been for her golden warrior? If so, he was lucky the castle healer had sought her out. He should be dead.

Shona removed his kilt to be sure there were no injuries elsewhere. She was very good about not looking *there*—even as she washed him. She glided the soap and linen from his toes to the top of his head, trembling fingers smoothing over corded muscle and strength. Nettles, but he was built like a tower—strong, sturdy and full of tight ridges.

The man was causing her to have odd reactions she'd do best not to have—especially considering he was out cold and injured.

Once he was clean, and his middle covered with a blanket, she went about rubbing his wounds with her medicinal salve. She sterilized her needle, looped it with the horsehair thread and then went to work. First, she sewed the cut on his head, sucking in a breath when he shifted and she nearly caused him a new slice.

"Be still," she crooned.

He barely made a sound while she worked, only the occasional grunt. Time passed, she wasn't certain how long, but her fingers were stiff and sore when she was done. She spread bog moss over the wounds and wrapped him in linen bandages.

Finally finished caring for his wounds, Shona cleaned up the extra linens and medicinal salves. She glanced at her patient and was startled to find that his heavily-lidded blue gaze was fixed upon her.

"Ye're beautiful." A genuine smile curled his lips.

"Thank ye," Shona murmured, heat filling her face.

Goodness, but was the warrior going to flirt with her while he lay injured upon her bed?

"Where am I?"

She flicked her gaze back to him again, noting that he was attempting to sit up, his brow wrinkled and lips turned down. Hands outstretched, she rushed forward and gently pressed him back onto the bed, trying to ignore the strength in his shoulders, despite his current condition.

"Do not move. Ye are safe here," she soothed.

"Is this your home?" He coughed then grimaced, the movement obviously causing him pain.

"Aye." She brushed his hair from his forehead. "Ye should lay still else your bandages come unraveled."

"What is your name?" He touched the bandage wrapped around his forehead and then the ones on his chest.

She watched him, prepared to swipe his hands away if he tried to undo the bindings. "Shona. Yours?"

"Ewan." His voice was stronger when he said his name.

Confident he'd not try to sit up again. Shona fixed him a soothing tea that would help ease his pain, keep fever at bay and make him sleep. She carried the cup forward and spooned drops into his mouth slowly so that he didn't choke. He parted his full lips, taking in the drink she offered.

"I'm not a bairn, I can drink on my own," he grumbled after the fact.

"Aye, I know ye can, Ewan," she said in a mollifying tone, then guided his hands to grip the cup, though she stayed close in case he needed her help.

As she'd noticed with some of her past charges, they didn't like to feel as though they'd completely lost all their faculties. What harm would it do allowing him to feel he had some strength left?

She studied him while he drank. His skin was pale, his lips white. He'd lost a lot of blood and the only thing that would bring it back was sleep, her herbal tisanes, and, when he was strong enough, some food.

"Rest well, warrior," she whispered, taking the cup from him.

But as she backed away from him, he gripped her arm and tugged her forward, his fingers sending a sizzle of something exciting rippling through her.

The cup fell from her hands hitting the floor and she gasped as he pulled harder, making her sprawl over his chest. Lucky for him, at the last minute, she was able to brace herself on either side of his arms so she wouldn't injure him further. *Daft man!*

Intent darkening his roving stare, a wicked tendril of heat shot through her, hitting every part of her body that she yearned for him to touch: lips, neck, breasts, thighs… slick sex.

"I'll rest better once ye kiss me," he rasped.

Her gaze met his cloudy one. The man was feverish. Mad from his wounds.

"We canna. Ye're hurt," she tried to argue, even as she leaned closer.

"What will a kiss do?" he asked.

But Shona wasn't sure if he, or even *she*, really understood the depth and breadth of that question. What *would* a kiss do? So very much.

Shona pressed her lips together, prepared to tell him nay, that they would never kiss, but he didn't wait for her to respond.

Warm lips brushed over hers. Soft and sweet. And even in their softness, something intense flared inside her. She gasped, and that moment when her mouth opened, he slid his tongue along the seam of her lips and then inside to tease the tip of her own.

"Ewan," she murmured. "We—"

But the stubborn man didn't let her finish. His hand threaded through the hair at the back of her head, holding her prisoner as he deepened the kiss, tangling their tongues and not allowing her to speak.

It was beautiful, delicious, so wanton. And she loved every single wicked stroke.

She would have kissed him all night into the next morning if she could. When his free hand slid over her ribs to cup her breast, she arched forward, wanting him to touch her aching nipple.

And that was when reality struck. What was she doing? She couldn't let him kiss her, touch her. What was she going to do—make love to a wounded man? That was unheard of. She'd lose all respect as a healer. She'd lose respect in herself for taking advantage of a man who'd barely made it out of the forest alive.

Still she kissed him. He certainly knew how to pleasure her mouth with his tongue. Zounds, but she liked this. Shona eagerly slid her tongue over his, one hand bracing her weight and the other palm scraping over the stubble on his cheek. She shivered at the sensations he evoked, moaned in the back of her throat when he massaged her breast and tweaked her nipple.

It'd been so long since she'd felt the pleasures of the flesh. So long since anyone had held her, kissed her, touched her.

She didn't want it to end, and while she'd allowed herself to indulge in the fantasy Ewan gifted her with, she knew she had to stop.

Probably *now*.

She pulled away gently, able to slide away from him in his weakened state.

"Forgive me," she whispered, guilt finding its way into every part of her.

"There is no need, lass, I enjoyed every minute of your seduction." He winked, a teasing smile curling his lips. "I hope ye're not offended."

"Never." That was the truth. If time could be turned back, she'd kiss him again.

Instead, she turned her back on him and said, "Sleep," while she reached for the jug of whisky.

After a lengthy pull on the bottle, her body still on fire from the Highlander's touch, she led the horse back outside to the small barn where a few other animals resided. The horse neighed his disgust, but she ignored him.

"Ye're lucky for not messing in my cottage," she said, though the threat was empty.

She got him situated in a stall, but a thought occurred to her as she touched the barn door. If someone were to come looking for the warrior, his horse would be easily recognized.

Shona bit her lip and returned to the massive animal. She made quick work with her knife—cutting the horse's mane. But even that didn't seem to be enough. She gathered some dirt from outside, mixed it with a touch of water, creating mud and smeared the brown sludge onto the black warhorse horse. She apologized all the while to the beautiful animal for her treatment.

Body still heated, she finished her task, and rushed back to her cottage—intent on never kissing the warrior again.

THE fire in the hearth popped and outside thunder crackled, lightning streaks making the inside of Shona's cottage white every so often. A summer storm was usually something she relished. She liked to leave the shutters ajar and look out as the sky went to war with itself. But she dared not open the shutters this night. Not with a strange warrior in her bed, and any number of people looking for him.

Whisky had made her belly warm, her head a little more quiet.

Since Ewan had been sleeping the past two hours, she'd done nothing but panic. Why had she allowed him to kiss her? Why did she take advantage of a wounded man? When would the MacDonalds who'd fought with him in the woods come to find her? When would his own men? The Grants would think she'd taken him for some nefarious purpose, after all they were not acquainted with her like the castle healers. Indeed, she'd heard the rumors. They called her the Witch of the Wood. Those same men would insist she meant to poison Ewan. His clan would believe she intended harm instead of aide—for why should she, unless she stood to gain something from it?

There was not a single thread of hope in her mind that she stood to benefit from what she'd done. If anything, the MacDonald men would match the arrows in her quiver to the one that had killed one of their men. Then they'd want to seek vengeance—to string her up—after torturing her.

"Oh saints, but what have I done?" she asked the silent room, her head falling against her palm.

She'd killed a man and saved a man.

She'd gone from practically anonymous forest dweller, to an idiot who shouted out their whereabouts by dragging a warrior who'd be missed to her cottage. She might as well have left a trail of red flags tied to the trees to lead them here.

Shona swiped her hand over her face and reached for the jug of whisky she normally used to clean infected wounds, and poured herself another dram.

Tossing it back, she didn't know whether to relish the burn of its path down her throat, or curse it. She supposed she ought to be happy that she was still alive, and not in the clutches of someone who wished to do her harm.

Relish it.

Rory's voice was so strong in her mind that Shona jerked around, expecting to see him standing behind her. But the room was empty save for the soft snores of her ward.

"Where are ye, Rory?" she asked the still air, just as she'd done a thousand times over the past two years.

Ewan grumbled, his arm flailing forward then falling limply at his side.

Had he come across Rory at some point in the wood? Thought Rory to be an enemy trespasser and dealt with him accordingly?

She prayed not, for she could never ask Rory's forgiveness if she tended to a man who'd seen to his demise.

Ewan flailed again, this time letting out a mighty shout.

"Blast." She shifted out of her chair, grabbed the whisky as she went and shuffled toward him, noting that four drams of the amber-colored liquid apparently made her toes a little numb. Slowing to a stop to steady herself, she took a deep breath and pushed onward.

"Drink up." She held the lip of the jug to his mouth.

Ewan's eyes flew up, the whites looking red in the firelight. Fever brewed in his body, she could sense it.

"Drink," she said again.

This time, his shaky hands closed over hers as he gripped the jug and swallowed.

"Och, that tastes like a horse's arse," he muttered.

Shona laughed. "Aye, but 'twill help ease your pain and your dreams."

"My dreams will never be eased with ye about," he said with a lop-sided grin and a lazy wink. "Let me kiss ye."

Shona worked hard not to roll her eyes and sink her lips to his. "Have another sip, warrior." She coached the jug back to his lips and watched him eagerly swallow. Zounds, but she wanted those lips on her own.

"Have ye a husband?" His hazy gaze roved over the tiny cottage. "Or are we all alone?"

All the mirth left her, as she stared down at the warrior. Searing heat wound its way around her middle, shooting down to her core and leaving her thighs to quiver. Why did his voice have to stroke the promise of pleasure over her sensitive body? "I've no husband."

Saying it out loud made her feel even lonelier than she'd felt before. And relieved that this man was here—even if she'd brought him here without his knowledge. All the same, he didn't seem to mind. In fact, he appeared to like her a little. *Nettles!* That was the whisky talking in her mind. The man was half mad with fever and her tincture!

"'Tis a shame, for ye're very bonny. I'd like to make love to ye, lass. Will ye let me?"

All the breath left her. Would she let him? How long had it been since she'd made love? Too long...

And she would like to let him. Would like to feel that wide mouth on hers, to savor the warmth of his lips brushing against her. To taste the whisky on his tongue and melt into his strong embrace. To have his body move over hers, between her thighs and inside her.

But he was injured. And she wasn't a harlot. The last thing she needed when his people finally figured out his whereabouts, was for them to brand her a whore, in addition to a witch.

"At least a kiss, love…" he crooned.

Nay, she'd not be labeled anything more than a loose wench if she let him touch her, and she knew in her soul she'd not stop him at a kiss. She'd let him touch her. Stroke her. Enter her, swift and hard.

Tingles pricked her skin, causing her nipples to harden and a twinge of pleasure to ignite between her thighs. Aye, she'd let him ravish her.

A mistake in itself. *Or a grand memory to carry me through the many years to come.*

Shona grinned slightly and shook her head. "I've not had enough whisky to allow a drunken, feverish Highlander to kiss me." How easy the lie had rolled off of her tongue—for not a few hours before she'd allowed it without a drop of whisky in her body.

"I am only fevered with my desire for ye," he said with a wiggle of his brows.

His fingers found their way to her arm and danced over the puckered flesh until he came to the crook of her elbow and made a little swirling motion that had her nearly gasping. She ached for him to make love to her, was filled with a feral need she'd not felt in many years.

She jerked away—surprised at how much he affected her and how much she wanted him to continue. "Ye know not what ye say."

Shona shoved away from the bed and stuffed the cork back into the jug. Best she not have anymore liquor, else she start believing a kiss from this warrior was worth it.

"Dinna leave me, lass, I'll behave."

Shona tossed a smile behind her then settled the jug onto a shelf, before returning to his side. "I'm not leaving, Ewan."

"Ye know my name?" he asked. "'Tis a shame, for I know not yours."

Her shoulders slumped. He did not remember her name. He obviously did not remember their kiss either. Likely he'd not even remember this conversation. Which was a blessing, but saddened her all the same.

"I am Shona," she said.

"Shona…" he whispered, trailing off.

With a tentative glance, she saw that he'd fallen asleep again with a smile on his lips. She was half-tempted to go and kiss him then, to know that he slept and wouldn't feel it or remember it, but that *she* would.

Before the urge grew too strong, she pushed away from him and tugged at the loaf of bread she'd been warming on a rock in the hearth. She ripped off a chunk, shoving it into her mouth.

The warm bread smoothed over her tongue and filled her belly, soaking up some of the whisky. She set aside a generous portion for the warrior in case he woke in the night hungry, though she doubted he'd be ready to eat until the morning, and then he'd do best with broth.

Having tended to him, she'd not had time to make the stew she'd planned, and so her supper consisted of the bread, a handful of roasted chestnuts she kept stored, an apple and tall cup of goat's milk.

Her belly full of food—and considerably less whisky—exhaustion began warring with her need to stay awake to keep an eye on her ward.

She supposed it couldn't hurt to sleep at least a little bit. Frowning at her bed occupied by a giant, she grabbed Rory's rolled up pallet and a plaid blanket from the trunk and set up her makeshift bed by the hearth. She'd already divested Ewan of his weapons when she undressed him and bathed him, storing the swords, *sgian dubh* and daggers inside the chest, though she kept a wicked looking dagger for herself. For protection.

She snuffed out the candle and laid upon the floor, staring into the last few dying embers in the hearth.

The storm had most likely chilled the summer air, but inside the cottage was cozy. Shona rolled onto her back, flopping an arm over her eyes. But every time she felt she was ready to fall asleep, a vision of the warrior's lips pressing onto hers, his body covering her with rigid hardness, would jolt her awake.

The visions were so intense, she couldn't decide if they were simply her desires coupled with whisky, or if she'd suddenly gained the sight.

Never had she desired to kiss a man as she did Ewan. Odd, too, because she barely knew the man. But just one look at his mouth, and the enticing words he said to her, the way his mouth had moved over hers before—she knew he would be a very good lover. He would please her to no end.

She blew out an annoyed huff and shoved all thoughts of the wicked Highlander from her mind. He might have been talking about kissing and making love tonight, but judging by the redness in his eyes, he'd only be begging for mercy on the morrow as fever waged a battle inside his body.

And for that battle, she needed to be prepared.

WAS he back at Hildie's?

Ewan lay upon a small, soft bed in a darkened room, but judging from the scent of the place, he was not at the debauched inn where a man's deepest desires were promised to come true.

Nay, this place had a mixture of smells that were foreign to him. Faintly floral, herbal. There was also a tang of blood and whisky.

"Where am I?" he croaked.

There was a rustling from somewhere in the dark.

"Ye are safe," crooned a soft voice. Like that of an angel.

Though he couldn't see her, he was instantly warmed by her. Did he know her? He didn't feel afraid of her. A ribbon of recognition wound around her voice.

"Who are ye?" he asked.

There was a sad sigh, and then more shuffling. Should he have known who she was?

"It doesna matter who I am," she said, then he felt the coolness of a cup at his lips and a bitter herbal tisane flowed into his mouth.

He sputtered.

"Dinna spit it out," she warned.

Ewan gritted his teeth and swallowed. "Are ye trying to kill me?" he asked.

She laughed, a sweet tinkling sound he wouldn't have minded hearing again. She moved away from him and he wished to call her back.

"Sleep, warrior."

"Sleep?"

"Aye, 'tis night, and ye need your rest."

Ewan was not used to taking directions from anyone but his laird, so it was odd to him that his eyes simply closed and his body prepared to sleep once more.

"Nay," he said, more to himself than to his fae warden. "I will not."

Another sigh came from several feet away—though this time she wasn't so much sad, as she was annoyed.

"Suit yourself, but ye'll have a wicked time in healing enough to be on your way if ye ignore your body's demand for sleep."

He raised his eyebrow skeptically in the dark. "How do ye know what my body needs?"

As the words left his mouth—and she gasped—he realized exactly what he'd said could be taken another way. But before he could yank back his words and explain himself, she answered.

"I am a healer. I seem to know more about a man's body than even a man. The lot of ye keep getting yourselves nearly killed, causing me to lose many night's sleep. Now I've got ye here, and ye're all sewed up. So get some rest, else ye take away another few hours of rest I so dearly need."

Ewan frowned. He didn't want to take away anything she needed. In fact, he felt an overwhelming urge to give her *everything* she needed or wanted.

That made him frown all the more. Who was she to make him feel such things? Must be the tisane. He felt sotted. That was it. Was thoroughly into his cups.

Aye, he'd had more than the tisane—he smelled whisky, too. Ewan realized the scent of it was on him, that her herbal mixture had washed away the remnants of it in his mouth. And he was glad of it, for all of the sudden, he started to feel each and every new wound.

"Go to sleep, Ewan," she said.

"Good night, Shona." Holy hell, he did know her name — and he'd not even been aware of it.

This time, a contented sigh filled the darkness.

CHAPTER FIVE

A clatter from outside woke Shona with a jolt.

Hand automatically reaching for the dagger she'd taken from Ewan, she sat straight up from her makeshift bed.

The fire had gone out completely, and only a little bit of light filtered through the shuttered window from outside.

But the sound was unmistakable.

Something — or rather *someone* — was outside.

A glance toward her bed showed that Ewan still slept. Thank goodness. Whoever was poking around outside would certainly hear him if he decided to thrash about and groan as he'd done periodically throughout the night.

With the dagger in one hand, she whipped back her woolen blanket with the other and swiftly, but quietly, came to her feet. Avoiding the furniture and various other objects, she tiptoed toward the door.

The noise came again—a shuffling sound and then, a bump against the outside wall.

Her breath hitched, heart pounded. Sweat glistened her palms.

No one—not even when Rory was alive—had ever come to the cottage with the intent of doing harm. Since he'd been gone, she'd been lonely, and had sometimes been afraid when the wind particularly howled, but never as much as she had since bringing the warrior into her home.

'Twas his fault she felt so unsafe, so out of her skin.

But all thoughts of blame quickly dissipated with the next nudge at the door.

Someone was trying to get in.

Shona pressed her free hand to the bar, not that if someone wanted to bang down her door the bar would do much good.

Rising up on her tiptoes, she moved aside a tiny slat of wood and peered through the small hole that Rory had carved for just such instances. Typically, her visitor would be one of the healers from the castle or a nearby village. But she saw no one.

And then a massive blur of black and brown swung before the hole, and a horse neighed from the other side.

Saints! They would have their horse kick down the door?

As if hearing her thoughts, a swift *thump-thump-thump* sounded at the base of her door.

Shona remained silent, not willing to even breathe. With no fire to cause smoke to curl from her chimney, they wouldn't know she was within. Though her few animals in the barn may give away that someone lived here—and blast it, but the warrior's horse was in there, too!

The blur of black and brown again, and then a puff of fetid air pushed through the hole.

Shona scrunched up her face and coughed.

Horse breath.

And three more kicks.

The tiny hole was not big enough to see what was truly happening beyond her door. No one spoke to her, 'twas as if they simply waited for her to make her presence known. Sheathing the dagger in her belt, she picked up a stool and took it toward her shuttered window. When Rory had built the cottage, he'd made certain the windows were sufficiently high up and small enough that no one could easily climb inside them. Windows were made for light—not for entry. She completely agreed.

And now she needed to see just exactly what was happening.

71

Shona carefully climbed on top of the stool and closed her eyes as she cracked the shutter, wincing at the tiny creaking sound and imagining whoever stood outside jumping in front of her to shout out, *"We've got ye now."*

No one shouted. In fact, only the horse nickered.

"What in god's name?" she murmured. "Horse?"

Ewan's horse stood at the door — and knocked — as if begging entry. He was still covered in mud. She'd given quite a hacking to his once luscious mane, and he no longer looked as noble as he truly was. He was completely alone — at least that was how it looked. Shona scanned her grounds and saw no one.

But, how had he gotten out?

She peered toward the barn but could only see a corner of it. Shona frowned. What did she expect of the warrior's horse? He could perform various tricks if issued the right Gaelic command. And here he was at her door, most likely intent on checking in on his master.

Blowing out an annoyed huff, Shona jumped down from her chair and moved to lift the bar. As soon as she had the door open, the horse barged his way in and, as if he owned the place, sauntered over toward the bed where Ewan slept.

Shona re-barred the door then followed the horse to the bed, and grabbed onto the reins before he could nudge the sleeping man.

"Leave him be," she muttered.

But the horse managed to stretch his neck just far enough forward to press his muzzle against Ewan's cheek for a brief second before she could tug him back.

"Did ye see her?" Ewan asked, a smile touching his lips. "A fair maiden, just for me, Bhaltair. Do ye think she'll cast a spell on me and then ravish me? A man can hope can he not?"

The horse preened at hearing his name — raising his head, lips pulled back, forelegs stomping and a gleeful whinny. Shona pressed her lips together to keep from laughing.

"Ah, Bhaltair, where have ye been? Did she take ye away from me?" Ewan rolled his head toward the both of them and opened his eyes. "Ye look a fright, my noble steed."

A smile covered Ewan's lips that she'd not seen before — not that she'd known him long. 'Twas the smile a father often gave a child, or a brother to his sister, an indulgent curl of lips.

She was envious of that smile. Covetous of what it meant. When she'd first arrived in Inverness some years ago, she'd been lost, alone, and without a memory of much. That's when she'd found Rory, and he'd tried to help her remember. Some things had come back to her slowly — others just naturally present, like her abilities with herbs and the knowledge that she enjoyed the touch of a man.

But one thing she'd not been able to shake was the incessant loneliness in her heart. Wherever she'd come from, she'd been alone there, too, she was certain of it.

Perhaps that was one of the reasons that made having Rory around so wonderful. A constant companion. A true confidant to hear her woes and cheer her on when she accomplished something new.

Tears stung her eyes.

Rory deserved so much more than what fate had offered him.

There was no way he would have simply left her alone. None at all. She refused to believe it.

Discreetly swiping at her tears, she said, "Your horse's name is Bhaltair?"

The horse bobbed his head at the mention of his name, and Ewan glanced at her. "Aye. And ye are the maiden."

Shona smiled through her sadness. "I promise not to lay a spell on ye, nor to ravish ye."

The warrior winked, his lip curling in a sinful grin. "Och, but dinna ye know? 'Tis what I want, lassie, for a beautiful maiden to ravish me."

Shona waved away his words, bending forward to press the back of her hand to his forehead. He was warm, not burning up quite yet, but definitely a low-grade fever. "I'll get ye an herbal drink for your fever."

Ewan pressed his hand to his heart. "Ye see, Bhaltair, my wish will come true!"

"Out with ye now, horse." Shona tried her best to give a stern look to her wounded warrior. "No animals in the cottage."

Ewan grunted, then laughed, though he ended up gasping in pain. "What happened? Why do I hurt so damn much?"

"There was a battle. Ye won."

"If this is what winning feels like—"

"The losers are dead." There was no need to tell him that a single MacDonald had gotten away. With his fever—and the possibility of it getting worse—the last thing she needed was dreams of battle and enclosing enemies to cause him to lash out and make a ruckus that would only draw them closer.

"Bhaltair," he said, squeezing his eyes shut. "Go, *rach*. Let the fairy take ye." The last of his words were whispered so quiet, she could barely make them out.

But his mount understood, heading back toward the door. If she didn't know better, she might have thought the horse was a man re-embodied.

Shona led the horse back to the barn, careful to inspect her surroundings. When she had him secure, she'd check on her traps, too. 'Twas too bad when Rory left that he'd taken their wolfhound Stretch with him. He was a great guard dog. Another reason why she was certain he must have come across something foul. Stretch would have fought to protect Rory, and then come home to find her if he couldn't.

In the barn, she could see that Bhaltair had somehow managed to open the gate to his stall. She wasn't surprised, more than she was annoyed.

This time when she put him in there, she blocked his gate with a bench. She'd made sure he had sufficient

75

water and oats from a lovely supply that she'd been paid in for her services.

"Be a good horse and stay put this time," she said.

She checked on her other animals — a pig, a goat and a few chickens that roamed. All looked to be fine, and had plenty of food to munch.

Next on her rounds were the woods surrounding her cottage. She tugged the dagger from her belt and held it tight, wishing she'd brought her bow and arrows with her, and thinking twice about going back inside to get them. There would be both MacDonald and Grant warriors out looking for Ewan. She would do best not to roam outside without proper protection. Decision made, she hurried back to the cottage to grab her bow and quiver.

Ewan still slumbered soundly, a soft snore every few breaths. With her quiver tossed over her shoulder, an arrow nocked in her bow, she carefully exited the cottage, closing the door behind her. Her heart pounded, feeling like it would come up into her throat. Shona paused just outside her threshold and took several deep breaths.

"Be strong," she murmured to herself.

She was brave. She was strong. If anyone wanted to trespass on her grounds, she'd put an arrow in them and ask questions later.

Well, maybe not. If it were one of the local healers, she'd not shoot them. But if it were a MacDonald, she definitely would. If it were a Grant? She wasn't certain.

Shooting one of the Grants would only get the laird angry with her. And she didn't want that. After all, she had to remain at the cottage, and so far he'd kindly ignored her presence.

At least she had some leverage. Ewan could always be used for a bargaining chip—her life for his. She just wanted to be left in peace.

An annoying tug pulled at her heart. She didn't want to be alone in her peace. Aye, she desired peace and happiness, but rather she sought it with a companion. She craved love. And despite his silliness in his fever, Ewan struck a chord inside her. Made her feel things she'd longed for, sparked a hope that had long since been buried. If he left, then she'd never know exactly what it was she wanted from him.

Shona marched carefully through the surrounding wood, jumping every time a squirrel scurried up a tree, or a bird flew from a branch, crunching the leaves and limbs.

By the time she got back to her cottage, she'd thoroughly wound herself up—and found nothing in the process, save for a rabbit to cook her stew. Though no warriors or outlaws had been out there this time, she wasn't naïve enough to believe that eventually someone wouldn't be knocking at her door.

Her stomach growled, reminding her she'd barely eaten any supper, and if she was going to have a delicious stew by this evening, she'd best get on with preparing it. The broth of the stew would help Ewan heal, too.

Shona opened the door to her little house and stepped inside, stunned to see Ewan standing—naked—in the middle of the room. Her heart leapt to her throat, her bow fell to her side. She was speechless as she regarded him, trying hard not to let her stare wander downward.

He held his sword straight toward her. Sweat soaked his entirely nude skin. She kept her eyes on his, afraid to see the impressive length of his cock—which she'd already witnessed while cleaning him—and from her peripheral vision was proudly jutting toward her.

"Who are ye and what have ye done to me?"

Shona ignored him, her eyes roving over the bandages to check for any blood seepage. Thank the saints, they'd not reopened, but she would need to clean them and rub a fresh salve on them once she got him to calm down and lay back on the bed.

She met his feverish gaze—eyes red and cheeks flushed.

"I am Shona, do ye not remember? I saved ye."

A grin curled his lips, but not like the ones he'd given her before, not sweet or full of desire. This was wicked and full of lust—and rage. She immediately felt as though he'd wrenched off her clothes to fully expose her. She shivered.

"There is one thing that would make me feel better—that would take away this awful ache in my head," he murmured, dropping his sword to his side, stabbing the point into the wood of her floor and stepping forward.

Shona's heartbeat leapt. Oh, dear lord... "What?" her voice came out breathless.

All she could think about was being hauled up against his hard body and repeating that steamy, toe-curling kiss.

CHAPTER SIX

THE world was spinning.

Ewan managed to stay standing despite the dizziness clouding his mind. A vision stood before him. Wild auburn hair, a beautiful face illuminated by sunshine.

Her gown looked worn, but clean, and her eyes were wide with a mixture of fear and lust. Blood surged to his cock, as his body spontaneously responded to the hunger she tried to hide.

He should answer her—put her at ease. He should tell her that a healthy serving of whisky would make him feel a hell of a lot better. But the way she looked at him... The way her eyes kept flicking to his lips, the way she so obviously tried not to look at his thick erection, he wondered if she thought he might want to ravish her — and if she wanted him to.

Why did he feel as though he'd dreamed of a kiss before? He was confused about where he was, about who she was, and yet she was familiar to him.

Ewan didn't like this feeling of uncertainty. He didn't like the shake in his legs either.

"Whisky," he said, his voice coming out rough. "I need a drink."

There was a flicker of disappointment on her face, and then relief. Ewan frowned. He might have ravished her — but only if she wanted. And it had appeared that was what she wanted, and yet she'd looked reassured? What could that mean?

Seeing this, the surge of heat in his blood dissipated to a dull roar he could mostly ignore.

Shona nodded, more to herself than him with her gaze flitting about the room. She closed the door and scooted around him, placing a skinned rabbit on a hook near the hearth.

She could hunt? The woman must have been skilled with a bow. A flash of memory from the woods assaulted him. He saw her. He saw his enemy dead at his feet, an arrow in his chest.

"How does your head feel?" she asked, pouring potent amber liquor into a cup.

"It aches something fierce." He studied her features.

The lass shifted on her feet, and seemed to have a hard time meeting his gaze. She was on edge.

When she handed him the cup, his fingers brushed over hers and a jolt went through him. Heat filled his blood and coursed a path down his body straight to his groin. *Ballocks*! A vivid memory flashed of her body rocking against him, his hand cupping her breast, a soft moan from her lips. His cock jumped, jutting between them like a lance.

'Twas then he recalled his nudity. But he didn't care. Whoever she was, her face colored red, and he found he liked it. Liked that she licked her lips, excited about his rising arousal. Liked that she tried to hide it behind a modest and demure façade.

Ewan chugged the whisky, keeping his eyes locked on hers, and handed her back the cup. "More, please, lass."

Och, but he sounded terrible. His voice was rough and cracked with disuse.

Shona said not a word but filled his cup with another dram, holding the jug to her chest as though she waited for him to ask for another refill. Which he did.

When he'd had his fourth, she shook her head.

"Ye've eaten nothing since ye've been here. Afore I let ye drink another drop, ye'll need to eat." This time her gaze did plunge, eyes widening as they took in the sight of his engorged shaft. Her lips parted as she let out a proper gasp and then quickly clamped closed. But she couldn't hide the swift surge of need that tingled between the two of them. "And get ye covered."

She yanked her gaze away from him and hustled toward the bed, grabbing up the plaid blanket there. He liked how she played at being a maiden, but he'd seen the lust light her gaze. And how was it he could recall her tongue sliding against his?

"Or, if ye like, ye can undress and we'll both be naked," he teased with a chuckle.

The lass snapped her eyes back to his and put her hands on her hips. "Ye're in no shape for such... such... sport."

"And, if I was, would ye?"

Her mouth fell open in what he supposed she hoped was outrage, but curiosity flared in her eyes.

Ewan grinned and nodded. "Ye would," he drawled.

But before she could respond, he swayed on his feet, the wooziness returning. He swung his arms out to steady himself, dropping the sword as he did so. Hell and damnation, but he was weaker than he thought. More feeble than he wished. Ewan glanced at the lass, hoping she hadn't noticed too much that he tottered like a wee bairn.

Shona watched him with narrowed eyes.

Ballocks! He did not want to appear frail to the woman he hoped to seduce. That would not help his cause at all.

He stumbled backward, grappling for purchase against the wooden table. Tiny stars danced in his vision. He squeezed his eyes shut, trying to rid himself of his dizziness and to clear his sight, but it didn't work.

He heard a clink as she set his sword on the table and then a warm hand slid over his back to his arm.

"Come, I'll take ye back to bed."

Ewan wanted to be strong. He stood straight, forcing himself not to sway, though the room still tilted and whirled.

"I'll allow ye to lead me, but only because ye're a bossy wench." His voice came out strong, which made him proud. He wrapped her arm tighter through his own—for her comfort.

"As ye say, warrior. Now come lay down and I'll bring ye some broth."

"Will ye be laying with me?" He glanced down at Shona and winked.

She clucked her tongue and gave him a stern look, though the curve at the corners of her lips did not seem too severe. He raked his gaze over her curvy form—luscious in all the right places.

Ewan lay back against the bed and the lass quickly swung a blanket over him, covering his nakedness, and his arousal. If he'd not seen her veiled interest, he might have thought she was embarrassed by the sight of his flesh—his rigid cock. But he knew better. A fire had burned in her gaze, and even now, he could see that her nipples were hard, pushing against her gown.

He reached out to touch her, but she jerked out of his reach.

Pity. He had a feeling her breasts would be warm and soft.

Shona muttered "broth," and whirled on her heel.

She crossed the tiny one-room cottage, swigging the whisky as she went. Ah, a lass who could drink like a man. That made him smile. She set the jug a little too hard onto the shelf and several of the other containers there clanked together. Her hands flew up as she scrambled to keep them all from falling.

Ewan couldn't help but smile. She was delectable. And damned seductive.

He sighed. Then frowned. The whisky on an empty belly was making him act a fool. He needed to compose himself.

"Ye've still not told me where I am," he said. From when he'd glanced out the window, he determined he was in the middle of nowhere. Castle Gealach could have been five or five hundred.

Shona peeked over at him, a coy look on her face and her shoulder shrugged, teasing. "In the woods."

The wench was toying with him. "I gathered that from the look of things outside."

"Did ye go out the door?" Her gaze darted toward the exit. She sounded surprised, concerned, filled with fear. He watched her hurry to make sure the bar on the door was secure and then she checked the windows, too.

What was this lass about?

"Nay. I made use of your windows."

She let out a great sigh of relief.

"What is out there? *Who* is out there?" he asked, curiosity filling him. "How did ye get me here, if ye saved me as ye say?"

Shona shook her head. "There is no one, yet. Your horse helped me."

"Bhaltair?"

"Aye. He's in the barn." She flicked her gaze toward the door, biting her lip, then turned back to her task.

"Is he well?"

A short laugh escaped her. "Aye, he is well. And well trained by ye, too. I'd not have been able to save ye without him, ye know."

"He is a good horse. Have ye an extra carrot or two to spoil him with?"

She smiled. "He's been spoiled plenty."

"Thank ye."

"Ye've no need to thank me."

"Aye, but I do. 'Tis not everyday a lass saves me in the wood."

"'Haps not."

"Ye said no one is outside *yet*. Who is coming?" Beautiful women did not live alone.

The lass had an obvious habit of licking her lip when she was nervous — and she was doing it now.

Shona walked forward with a bowl full of broth, setting it down to prop up his pillows. "No one we want. Do ye think ye can manage or shall I feed it to ye?"

He rather liked the sound of her feeding him, but he suspected she'd think him a completely weak fool. Already he lay wounded, dizzy, and out of sorts within her home.

Ewan took the offered bowl and brought it to his lips. As the warm broth slid down his throat, he closed his eyes in enjoyment. 'Twas the best tasting thing to ever cross his tongue. Though he suspected starving and drunk on whisky, desire and the fever that heated his blood, he might think a pile of dirt tasted heavenly.

"Sip it slowly," she said.

Ewan studied her over the bowl as he drank. Her fiery-colored hair was plaited, but stray locks had escaped in unruly waves around her face. Her skin was smooth, free of wrinkles. Eyes the color of almonds. She watched him watching her, her lips in a flat straight line.

"What are ye thinking?" he asked.

Shona looked taken aback. "I'm thinking of naught."

"Ye lie." He said it quietly as he scrutinized her through the whisky haze.

She took a step back as though she'd been slapped. "How dare ye accuse me of lying after I've taken care of your wounds and kept ye safe. I fed ye from my own pot."

Ewan shook his head and smiled, imploring her with a hand to come closer. "Ye mistake my meaning, lass. I'm not calling ye a liar, but merely that ye didna tell me the truth."

She stayed rooted in her spot. "Are they not one and the same?"

"Nay, they are not."

"I disagree." Shona crossed her arms over her chest.

Their banter only made Ewan smile wider. "I disagree with your disagreement."

Shona huffed and turned away from him. "Finish your broth. I'm going to get the salve ready to change your bandages."

"Och, ye dinna need to do that. I'll be perfectly well without it."

She whipped around, a brow raised and a hard glare in his direction. "Ye will not be well at all." She marched back toward him and pressed the back of her hand to his forehead. "Ye burn with fever."

Ewan leaned up further on his elbows than the pillows allowed, feeling like he burned with much more than a fever from his injuries. "But lying down did take away the light-headedness."

Shona groaned, took his empty bowl of broth and pushed him back on the bed. "Lie down."

"Aye, my lady." He gripped onto her wrist, feeling the pulse beat fast just below the surface.

Shona's gaze connected with his, and his own pulse leapt. "Humph. Ye know as well as I do that I'm no lady."

Ewan shrugged. "Makes no difference to me." He wanted to kiss her. To pull her on top of him, just like he'd dreamed of doing. The most heavenly dream it had been... He gave another little tug, but she slipped out of his reach.

"We'll not be doing that again," she said.

Ewan grinned. "So we've done it before?"

She glanced away from him. "I dinna know to what ye're referring."

"I think ye do, and I think ye liked it."

"Ye burn with fever. Ye'd think me a fairy floating on wings if ye wanted to."

Ewan grinned. "Perhaps I do."

"Hush now, ye need to rest." She was glowering at him, but the frown didn't wash away the spark of awareness hidden behind it.

"I thought ye were going to change my bandages?" He raised a brow in challenge.

Shona stomped toward a pile of folded linens and grabbed them along with two jars. When she returned to him, her creamy face was colored red.

Lord, she was gorgeous.

HE was wicked.

And she was weak.

Shona wanted nothing more than to crawl over top of Ewan and let him kiss her. To feel the length of his arousal grow thick and press between her thighs. To feel his breath on her lips, his hands on her breasts, his tongue stroking fast then slow over her trembling flesh.

She licked her lips, watched his eyes flick toward her mouth.

He was flushed with fever — or desire — she couldn't be sure which. Probably a bit of both. But it didn't really matter. He was her patient and she needed to take care of him, not think of seducing him, or even repeating their little kiss. Nettles, but it wasn't a little kiss…

Shona drew in a deep breath and pushed her desire aside. "Please, put your arms over your head."

God help her, the wicked man winked. "Are ye going to tie them to the bedpost? Is that what ye like, lass?"

The last of his words were slurred, the whisky and fever combined having taken away his faculties. But even still, the image he evoked in her mind was enough to make her shudder.

She'd not tied a man to a bedpost before, let alone been tied to one herself, but the idea did something funny to her insides. 'Twas potent and overpowering.

Intense curiosity filled her. What would it be like to be restrained? To be full of desire, heat and primal need — and unable to get it.

A shiver stole over her. Her nipples hardened, and between her thighs dampened. Her teeth clamped down on her lip as she kept herself from asking if he minded trying it out.

"Arms, over your head," she ordered, her voice a little shaky.

"An overbearing chit. I do like them that way."

"I care not," she said. Though the heavy ache in her breasts and increasing pressure in her core suggested otherwise. "Sip this."

She handed him a small vial filled with an herbal tincture that would induce sleep and take away some of his pain. Once he'd drained the vial, she set it aside and removed his bandages and the bog moss, taking note that all bleeding had stopped. The salve she'd used before had dissolved inside his wounds. The edges of his wounds were an angry red, but not inflamed. There was every indication that he was, in fact, healing.

"Ye look to be healing well," she murmured.

Ewan glanced down his torso, riddled with old and new wounds.

"Does it bother ye?" he asked.

He regarded her warily, worry and self-consciousness showing on his face. Shona didn't want him to feel that way around her. She wanted him to be comfortable.

"I've seen many men wounded." She kept all emotion from her voice. She'd not tell him that his wounds and scars in particular had bothered her, only because she'd worried so much for his safety and wondered what kind of life he could have led where he was always being injured.

Always in pain.

"Any as torn up as me?" he asked.

91

Shona smiled and squeezed his shoulder. "Many just like ye. Ye warriors are a sad and sorry lot, always asking enemies to slice and dice at ye. But ye're not ashamed of your scars are ye? Are they not wounds ye can boast about amid your warrior friends?"

A sad smile crossed his lips. "Sometimes. Others I rather wish had never happened."

"'Haps one day ye can tell me about them?" She rubbed a freshly boiled linen onto his wounds, pulling away any lingering infection and then smoothed on a fresh layer of salve, covered it with bog moss and new, clean linens.

"'Haps, though I'd rather leave such cruel memories where they belong." His lips curled into a frown.

Shona cocked her head with interest. "And where is that?"

He made a *poofing* sound, pinching his fingers and then widening them for effect. "Nowhere."

She finished wrapping up the last of his wounds. "But do we not learn from our memories, good or bad?"

"Hmm. Aye. I've learned a lot, lass."

"'Haps more than a man should?" She put the lids back on her jars and returned them to her shelf.

Ewan sighed deeply, his eyelids drooping. Good. The tincture was working.

"I gladly accept any trial the lord seems fit to give me."

Shona pulled the blanket up over his chest, touched her hand to his cheek.

"Ye'll be rewarded for your bravery."

"I think I already have been," he said with a genuine, infectious smile.

Shona found herself grinning back—her hand still cupping his face.

His eyes closed and a soft snore blew past his lips. While he slept, Shona took the time to wash his hair, her fingers sliding through the golden mass, massaging his scalp—careful to avoid his injury. When she was done, she brushed it until it was nearly dry and imagined what it would be like if Ewan lived here, with her, always.

CHAPTER SEVEN

THE cottage was filled with the scents of stew and Ewan's nightmare-filled cries.

He thrashed about on the bed while Shona tried to tidy up. When she couldn't stop herself from checking him for fever, and watching him as though he'd wake and beg for another kiss, she decided it was time to take care of the animals. If only she could take his mount out for a ride. They'd both most likely enjoy the exercise, but leaving the vicinity of the cottage wasn't a choice she had.

If something were to happen to Ewan while she was gone, she'd never be able to forgive herself. When she'd dragged him onto that horse and taken him home, she'd claimed responsibility for him — at least until he was well. And it had nothing to do with his sinful lips or heated touch. Nothing at all. Whatsoever.

Shona frowned. Aye, she had to get out of this cottage, if only for a few minutes to give herself some air. Might help the headache she'd developed from drinking too much whisky the night before.

'Twould also be good to air out the cottage. If fresh air could help her headache, it would likely help Ewan as well. She opened the shutters on the two windows, shafts of dull light and a subtle breeze flowing in.

Gathering up some apples and scraps in a bowl that she'd saved for the animals, Shona took the treats out to the barn.

Bhaltair whinnied when she entered and kicked at his stall gate.

"I know ye want out of there, beast, but I canna let ye." She handed him an apple as a peace offering, which seemed to work for a moment, then he was bobbing his head toward the door. "Well, 'haps just a walk around the yard."

Shona lifted Bhaltair's bridle and reins from the hook on the wall, watching as the animal perked up at her movements. She slipped them in place and then opened the stall gate. He walked out, nuzzling her hair and lipping her shoulder. Stroking the animal's forehead, she said, "You're a good boy, are ye not?"

Bhaltair's tail flicked back and forth as they exited the barn and she led him around the yard, letting him nibble on grass. Overhead, the sky was still a fierce gray, and the sun was working hard to push through, but judging from the damp scent in the air, rain would be forthcoming. While Bhaltair snacked, Shona tugged a small tree she'd hacked down the day before toward the barn. She needed the wood for her fire, and would have to chop it shortly. Her supply was growing small. Though she didn't need much—especially in summer—it didn't hurt to get the pile growing for the coming winter. In fact, she was well behind in all her preparations. She'd need to go in search of nuts, wild apples and root vegetables for drying. Her first winter without Rory had been tough. The second, only slightly better. But she had a plan now of how to prepare, and she didn't want to repeat those hardships again.

Thank goodness her services as a healer and medicine maker had been good enough to keep work coming, and that people paid mostly in tangible goods.

The barrel beside the barn that Rory had set up to catch water when it rained, was near the brim. That needed to be taken care of, too. They had no well, and the nearest trickle of water was a good quarter mile away. If she ran out of water, that was quite a hike if treacherous weather didn't permit her to leave. Or, if she was housing a warrior and most likely considered an outlaw for having murdered a man.

Was it really murder if she'd been acting in the defense of Ewan, and herself?

She'd sent a prayer of forgiveness to the Lord, and knew he'd seen the circumstances. Besides, they'd not been found yet, that had to mean something, didn't it?

She worked to fill several buckets and jugs full of water that she could boil and store, then regrettably informed Bhaltair that grazing time was over. The warhorse seemed to understand and went willingly back into his stall.

Taking the rest of the scraps she'd brought out, Shona fed her pig and goat, making sure they all had fresh hay and water. Working in the barn and yard was calming, and she had started to feel somewhat normal again, even taking a moment to sit down on a stump and breathe in the fresh, rain-scented air, which helped to alleviate the pounding in her head.

When thunder rumbled overhead, she made her way back inside. Ewan still rested on the bed, and had quieted down, thank goodness. She checked on her stew, stirring it and adding in a few more savory herbs. Her stomach rumbled, but it wasn't quite ready. To stave her hunger, she boiled water and herbs, making herself a calming tea.

The first pings of rain tapped against her roof, and with it the darkened clouds threatened to cover the sun. Shona closed the shutters against the rain and lit a candle, the soft golden glow lighting up the suddenly darkened room. The day or so of warm, dry weather had lost its battle with the storm clouds. She curled up on her makeshift bed in front of the fire. She'd only rest for a little while. There was still much she had to do that she'd not been able to get done the day before.

Ewan's soft snores lulled her into a state somewhere between consciousness and slumber. But complete quiet never came as her mind continued to question the man lying on her bed. What had happened to him? Something horrible, else he'd not have mentioned how much he *learned* from it. Had someone betrayed him? Was it punishment for something he, himself, had done?

If it weren't for the healing aspects of sleep, she might have woken him to find out more. But for now, she supposed the both of them would need to rest — that was, if sleep came to her.

Shona couldn't seem to get a handle on her mind, continuously thinking about Ewan and his kiss, his touch. She slammed her eyes closed and forced herself to not think about his wicked, swirling tongue.

The man was a mystery. Obviously one who'd lived a harsh and dangerous life. Did she truly want to get mixed up with a man like that? Already, she'd lost Rory, and they'd lived a quiet existence. But then, again, a kiss did not mean that she had to be his wife — that she had to live at the castle with him.

If that was where he lived. He'd said he was a Grant warrior, which meant he fought for their laird. But perhaps he was a lesser warrior within the laird's army, and he lived in the village. She could be a villager's wife. *Nay*! What was she thinking? The villagers were suspicious people. Frightened by herbs and the healing skills some women possessed. An enchantress, they'd call her. They'd want to string her up, to burn her. Punish her for their fears. She'd never be anything but, the Witch of the Wood.

Perhaps a kiss was a frightening thing. Men and women could fall under the spell of lust. Lose themselves in passion and forget just who they were. That was what happened to her when Ewan kissed her. She wanted things she couldn't have. Desired a life that was not hers.

An incredible, bone-deep sadness filled Shona. Partly because she wondered if she would live her life forever alone, and partly because if Rory were to come back—she'd not experience a kiss like Ewan's again. Nay, Rory wouldn't allow it—and Ewan would be lucky to survive their meeting.

AN hour later Shona still lay awake, sleep refusing her. She tossed back the covers. If sleep would not come, she'd best make good use of her time doing her chores. Her body was sore, muscles aching. She stretched tall, feeling those kinks work their way out.

Several herbs hung above her hearth where they'd been drying. They needed to be ground into powder and stored. She pulled them from their hooks and set them on the table, took a seat and filled her mortar bowl. The aroma of each herb she ground slowly with the pestle filled the air, rivaling her stew.

Outside the wind howled and thunder cracked, flashes of lighting made Shona's small cottage go bright then dim. How long would this summer rainstorm last?

The wind ripped open the shutters. Silver lightning flashed into the candlelit room.

The clatter of the shutters against the wall caused her charge to stir in his soundless sleep. Shona jumped from the chair and rushed toward the windows. She had to reach up high to shut them tight, tinkering with the iron clasps until each felt secure.

"Lass..." Behind her, Ewan called out, his voice raspy.

Glancing at him, she saw that he still slept. Perhaps he was dreaming. She did not want to disturb him. He needed to heal. Sleep, along with her remedies, was the best way to restore his body to health.

He shifted restlessly, one arm flopping over his face, and the other landing on his chest. A wince scrunched his sleeping face and he groaned. Shona moved slowly and quietly toward him, prepared to wake him if he pulled at his bandages.

Ewan's hands settled, and the flow of the hearth fire waved shadows over his stubbled cheeks. A sense of warmth filled her when she looked upon him. The man was a stranger to her, and yet, he was the only other human she'd connected to in this place besides Rory.

"Nay…" he muttered. "Nay, ye bloody…"

Shona turned from him, feeling as though she were encroaching on his private thoughts. She went back to her herbs, working extra hard to grind them. Ewan continued to mutter in his sleep, and she continued to pay him little attention. But, when he whispered her name, *that* she could not ignore.

Shona rushed to his side and bent over him, studying his complexion, which was still flushed. She put her hand to his forehead. Zounds, but he was not nearly as hot as he'd been before. Her tincture was working. Shona refilled the cup and brought it to his lips, catching the scent of the mint she'd used to flavor it.

"Drink," she said.

Ewan blinked open his eyes, and for the first time she noticed how light their color. An icy, sparkling blue, like the way she imagined a spring would look if ice-covered, or the purest blue of the summer sky. She was momentarily stunned by their beauty. Thick black lashes framed his eyes. She could have stared at him all day. In fact, she was probably already staring too much.

He took a sip, then his lips quirked into a grin — a wicked grin that had her body heating and caused a smile of her own to curve her lips. Her mind was suddenly filled with the taste of his mouth and her body yearned for him to touch her. How could he unnerve her in such a way? How could he command her body with just a grin?

Why did he look at her like that? And why did she like it?

"My healer," he rasped.

Shona nodded, glad that he seemed to be more aware, and that he recalled who she was. A definite sign of improvement. The warrior's gaze dipped to her lips, remaining there intently. Was he thinking about kissing her? On instinct, she wet her lips, suppressed a shudder. She should move, shouldn't be hovering over him like this. She was only enticing them both to something that should not happen again, no matter how much she wanted it.

Heaving a sigh, Shona set down his cup, but could not force herself to step away. Rather, it seemed she leaned closer. She sat on the bed beside him, liking the heat of his body sinking into her. And the way he was looking at her as though she were a morsel he'd like to devour. Interest, curiosity and the intense need curling in her belly kept her frozen in place.

"How long have I been here?" he asked.

"Not long. Only a couple of days," she whispered, unable to find her voice.

Her heart pounded. Breath caught.

Ewan's hands trailed up her arms and over her back sending ripples of heightened sensation racing along her spine. How did he know to touch her in just the right way? And why wasn't she yanking away, putting distance between them? This was wrong, wicked, wanton. And yet, she embraced it, because it also felt right.

"Was it ye with the arrows?" he asked, his gaze searching hers.

Seemed he was coming to his senses. Shona nodded, fearing if she spoke, the only sound that would come out was a soft pleading moan. He swirled slow, sensual circles at the base of her spine and on her hips. Did he realize how much his touch affected her?

"Ye're an angel." He leaned up, his face coming closer to hers and stealing her breath. "I've always wanted to kiss an angel."

Shona nodded, then quickly shook her head. The man was clearly still under the influence of her tea. He had to be, else he wouldn't truly want to kiss her, would he? It didn't matter, she couldn't let him kiss her again. But her lips seemed ever closer to his, and she couldn't pull away. Was frozen in place by his mesmerizing, whirling fingers and heated gaze. This was sinful. Kissing a man who didn't have his wits about him... But he appeared clearer than he'd been in the past couple of days.

"Let me kiss ye, Shona," he whispered, not more than a hair's breadth from her mouth.

He remembered her name, and the way he'd said it stroked away any last resistance she had. One more kiss could hardly hurt. "Ye know my name," she managed as their lips brushed.

Wicked heat wrapped around her middle, her nipples hardened, and gooseflesh rose along every inch of her skin. Between her thighs grew damp. Though most of her past memories were fuzzy at best, Shona was certain she'd never responded to a touch like she did when in Ewan's arms. She couldn't shake how wrong this was, but that it felt so right... There was no one here to judge her, only herself and the man who demanded her mouth's attention.

Just another kiss to remember him before he left, was found by his men, or worse by the enemies that lurked in the woods. His people had to be looking for him, though there had been no sign of anyone when she'd worked in the yard. Even still, that didn't mean they weren't lurking. They could knock at any moment. Within the hour, he could be torn from her embrace and forever a stranger to her. Knowing that seemed to only heighten her urgency. Shona threaded her fingers into his soft golden hair. Hair, she'd washed herself. Indeed, she'd washed his entire body, felt his skin prickle as she'd glided the soapy cloth over his taut, muscled flesh — and felt her own flesh tingle in response. She'd been good about keeping him clean, aware that when the fever caused him to sweat she needed to wipe away those tainted drops.

She could still smell the soap on him. Could taste the mint on his tongue. If she kept her eyes closed, she might even be able to imagine that he was not wounded. That he was not here in her cottage because she'd brought him here to take care of him, but because he'd pursued her. Because he wanted her.

The thought of him desiring her as much as she yearned for him sent a rush of excitement and delicious sensations through her.

Raindrops made repeated dull thuds on the thatched roof, and the moist scents of rain mixed with Ewan's raw, masculine aura. Shona let herself sink further into him. The slide of his tongue over the seam of her lips made her gasp and open her mouth. But he didn't invade. Didn't thrust his tongue in. Nay, he teased her, darting in and out, swiping, twining. She couldn't draw a decent breath.

One hand slid hotly over the curve of her buttocks and the other trailed up her ribs, over her shoulder and to her throat. A thumb on one side of her neck, his fingers on the other, he pressed. A flash of panic snagged her as he gently squeezed. Her pulse quickened along with her breath. Maybe she should have been scared. Should have pulled back, but for some reason, this man's small show of dominance sent her body into a somersault of pleasure.

Instead of pushing him away, Shona climbed over his body, bracing her weight on her arms, their pelvises collided as she slid her long legs on top of his, careful to keep her weight off his injured torso. Her breath hitched as another whirl of decadent pleasure shocked her. Ewan's cock was rock hard, long, and ground hotly against her, thrilling her.

The feel of him beneath her was exquisite. She opened her eyes, meeting his sky-blue stare. She stilled, chewed on her lower lip as they regarded one another.

"I dinna want to hurt ye," she said, suddenly aware of his state and what harm she could bring him. Nettles, but she should just get off of him, but she couldn't.

"Ye're not." His voice was gruffer than before, the sound of it raking sensually over her.

"But I might." All he had to do was give her a sign she was hurting him and she'd get off of him. Leave him be, sleep outside in the rain.

"Ye won't." All the wicked playfulness of Ewan was gone and replaced by an intense heat that made her shiver.

Why did this have to be so complicated?

Again his gaze searched hers.

She kept her eyes steady on his, wanted to open herself up to him, to let him see into her soul, to share her secrets. But the terror that thought brought on was enough to make her blood run cold.

"Shona... Is there anyone... here for ye?"

His question hit a chord deep inside, and she glanced away, not wanting to let in how isolated she truly was.

"I have no one," she whispered. And likely she never would, but she wasn't going to admit it to him. Did not want his pity, only his touch. She'd wanted to escape for the moment. To pretend she was someone else, and that he truly cared for her. Shona started to pull away, but Ewan pulled her back, surprisingly strong for his condition.

"Nay, lass, I'm here. Ye have me." He leaned up and scraped his teeth along her jawline, then slid his mouth over to hers. "Let me have ye."

Shona pressed her lips hard to his, drinking in his kiss with an urgency she wasn't quite sure how to control. "For tonight."

CHAPTER EIGHT

"AS ye say," Ewan whispered against the vixen's mouth.

She might have said only for tonight, but he'd not been able to get her out of his sleep-induced, feverish brain, and once his temperature had broken, her name was the first on his lips. He'd pretend for her that this was only one night, but in truth, he planned to pursue her in earnest.

Just days before, he'd been intent on remaining a bachelor—on frolicking with Hildie and her wenches for the rest of his days. He'd even balked at the idea of his laird marrying. Had teased Logan for his love and enjoyment of his wife. But he'd not realized how much he was missing until Shona had stepped into his life.

Not that he'd be telling her this.

She made him feel like he was not alone in the world. He'd not realized before how lonely he truly was. The moments with Hildie and any other willing lass had fleetingly assuaged his desolate existence, but... They weren't truly enough. And he wasn't certain if this was because he'd nearly died twice now in the span of six months and he wanted someone to remember him when he was gone, or if he was turning over a new leaf as Logan had. Admittedly, the latter scared the living hell out of him.

But he'd be a fool not to admit that there was a connection and bond between them both that begged to be examined. He didn't know what it was or how it was possible, but he wasn't going to let her go. He was going to fully explore her and the mysterious bond that held them tight. He'd leave no stone, nor inch of skin, unexplored. Aye, he was going to claim this nymph for himself.

"Promise me," she said, her hands cupping the sides of his face.

Ewan gripped her hips, massaging her as he lifted upward to grind his rigid cock against her warmth. "Anything," he said.

"Promise me this one night."

How could he deny her request and yet still appease his own desires? "I promise ye as many nights as ye wish."

"Just one."

"As ye say," he said once more. There was no way he could promise only one, and by answering this way, he was leaving them both open for more.

"Oh, Ewan, ye make me feel... hot, and, and, wanted," she murmured. Her velvet tongue slid inside his mouth to tangle with his.

"Lass, I want ye so bad, can ye not feel it?" He tilted his pelvis up again so she could feel just what he meant.

Surging heat seared his veins and skin. Never had he been so filled with need and passion. Was it *her* or her tea? Had to be her...

Shona responded to him by arching her back and thrusting her breasts forward. Ewan stroked his hands over the offered mounds. Soft globes with turgid peaks. The lass had perfect breasts and he wasn't sure she even knew it.

"Ye're so beautiful," he murmured. "And these are perfection." Ewan leaned upward to nuzzle her breasts, breathing over the puckered peaks, one at a time.

In her arms, every ache disappeared, and he was whole again.

Shona threaded her fingers into his hair again. He loved the feel of her hands on him, of the way she held him possessively. The woman was full of passion and he wasn't certain she knew that either. Furthermore, he was more than happy to be the one to unleash her fiery manner. In fact, he insisted upon it, though, he wasn't certain how long he'd last. She rocked back and forth on his hard cock. With only a blanket and flip of her skirts keeping him from entering her silken warmth, Ewan found any control he might have possessed slowly slipping away.

He nibbled on her nipple, reveling in the sound of her moan. "I like the sound of ye moaning, lass. I want to make ye moan all the more."

SHONA'S heart could burst from her chest it pounded with such fervor. What was he doing to her?

Ewan gripped the back of her neck and tugged her down for a hard, demanding, hot, claiming kiss, sending a thrill rushing through her. He explored her mouth with dizzying concentration, his hands on her breasts, then up and down her thighs as he skimmed them beneath her gown.

He slid his mouth over her chin to her ear, teasing her earlobe. Shona couldn't stop the continuous gasps and moans that kept rushing from her, but Ewan answered every one with a groan of his own. Their kisses, their touches, their responses, it was... she didn't know. All she was aware of was that she felt so darn good. Her skin was prickling, her blood rushing and between her thighs, wet and tingling. A delicious pressure slowly built inside her, and she moved with anticipation to scratch the itch.

Ewan continued to tease her ear. He sucked her skin, pushed it out with his tongue only to suck it back in. Her golden warrior was playful, a tease. He made her see red, every touch a sharp and penetrating dance into ecstasy. It floored her. Compelled her forward, to see just how much more he could make her feel.

Plain and simple, the man intoxicated her.

"Ye're skin is so soft," he said, trailing his fingers away from her neck to her collarbone. His mouth followed the path, pebbled flesh trailing his tongue. "And ye taste sweet as honey."

Shona rubbed the juncture of her thighs boldly over his engorged flesh. A daring and wild woman emerged from somewhere buried deep inside, startling her. "Mmm, and ye taste of mint." She pressed her nose to his neck, flicking her tongue out to taste his heady flesh.

Ewan tugged on the shoulder of her worn wool gown, skimming his fingers along the inside. Shona was suddenly hot, wanting desperately to disrobe. To make all her clothing go away, to toss his blanket to the floor and slide naked against his taut body.

"I... um..." She could barely talk. Overwhelming heat and delicious sensations darted through her body, causing her mind to skate from one thought to the next and all of them having to do with Ewan's kiss, his touch, and what the future held.

Fear collided with passion. She needed to put some distance between them. She needed to exhale, to think.

While she'd agreed to kiss him, agreed to be his for one night—had she been lucid when she agreed to make love to him? Or was she blinded by the sizzle of his touch? By the overwhelming need to connect with someone?

Did *he* even know what he asked? The man was coming back from the brink of death, could she really expect him to make good on a request such as this?

His fingers danced over her belly, her breasts, and he leaned up to pull down her gown, exposing one nipple to his mouth. Maybe he did know. And maybe she should let this be what it was—pleasure for one night only.

Her head fell back on a moan as his soft, warm mouth tugged and sucked at her sensitive flesh. The way he made her feel—hot and desirable—was likely enough to make her strip off all her clothes and declare herself his forever, even before she took her next breath. And though her curiosity, her desire, was piqued, it would be wrong to go through with it. Wouldn't it? Passion was what had brought them this far. Nothing lasting.

Except... There was one other thing that had brought her to this point. Need. The need to connect with another. The need to feel something other than loneliness, emptiness. Not until now had she realized truly how alone she'd been. And how could she ignore that?

Ewan's hand softly circled her abdomen, feather-light. Then he moved lower, just a hint of his hand cupping her sex, arousing her all the more — and he'd barely touched her. Shona gulped, waiting for more, but it appeared he was waiting for permission.

Could she give it when moments ago she'd decided she had to leave him alone?

"I canna do this," she said, regretting every word. "Ye're ill —"

"I'm nay so ill." He tilted his hips up, his cock rubbing along her sex and making her jump. "Nay so ill that I canna want ye. Pleasure ye."

Shona shivered. "Aye, but…" She gazed into his eyes, seeing them hazy with her herbal tincture and something more… They burned with longing. All fever had left him.

"No buts, sweetheart," he murmured. "I want to make love to ye. Do ye desire me?"

This man was offering something she'd not felt in so long — if ever — a moment's escape from her loneliness that she could forever hold inside her heart. She knew it wouldn't last. This was a one time thing. Was it worth the cost of her heart?

One look at his handsome face and the promise in the depths of his eyes and she was nodding.

More than worth it.

"Aye. Touch me," she whispered, against his lips, sucking his lower lip gently into her mouth.

His thumb rimmed her nipple again and again, and then brushed over the firm tip. A soft moan escaped her, and she arched into him, filling his hand with her breast, wanting him to lick her there once more. Thoughts of removing herself gone, she fully gave him everything she had.

Without warning, Shona crashed her lips down on his, not willing to let him let her off the hook. Aye, it was wrong to take advantage of him. Wrong for her to act the wanton. But she'd answer for those consequences later. For now, she wanted nothing more than to feel this Highlander's touch, to feel him sink inside her.

Ewan growled, thrusting his tongue inside her mouth, taking possession, ownership. Shona arched into him, rubbing her sparking nether-region against the rigidness of his cock. The sensations made her tremble, her entire body suddenly on fire. Fingers still threaded in his hair, she gripped hard, massaging the back of his scalp to take away the sting. Her need was intense, her plea potent enough to make lightning strike. Tonight, she was going to let go. She was going to give in to her desire, to her body's demand, and allow this warrior to give and take pleasure.

Lifting herself up so that she straddled his blanket-covered hips, Shona gripped her gown and tugged it over her head. Pulled off her chemise, letting the chill evening air hit her skin. Finally she was nude, her skin glowing in the candlelight, nearly as golden as his.

She swallowed hard, watching his gaze rove hungrily over her, feeling as though she was seeing herself for the first time through his eyes.

When he spoke, Ewan's voice was gravelly, thick. "Ye're even more beautiful than I could have imagined." He caressed over her belly, fingers sliding up tenderly to touch her breast. "I'm going to worship ye," he whispered, leaning up on his elbows.

Warm lips captured hers. Shona sank into him, wrapping her arms around his neck—but careful not to let her chest touch his injuries—she kissed him with every ounce of passion she possessed. The tips of her nipples brushed tantalizingly against the crisp hair on his chest, though she bowed her back to keep from hurting him.

Dragging his mouth from hers, Ewan kissed and licked her neck to her shoulder. He held her arm out to the side and slid his lips down to her elbow, tonguing the indentation there. Every part of her burned for him, even the space of flesh between her elbow and her wrist where he kissed her. The man didn't miss a finger. Tenderly kissed each knuckle and gently drew her fingertips into his mouth, teasing them with his silken tongue.

Shona shivered, moaned, her sex quickened, the aching pulse deep inside her grew until she writhed for more. Not a single inch of her was still, and not a single inch of her didn't crave his touch.

He caressed his way to her breasts, nuzzling around the plush mounds and taunting her before finally, flicking his tongue over the puckered flesh. He drew her nipple into his mouth, sucking. Hard.

Shona moaned, arching her back, her nails digging into the muscles of his shoulders. While he teased her breasts with his mouth, his fingers tracked a path to the thatch of hair between her thighs. He teased the folds, barely touching, just hovering, enough that she was panting and slick with the need to feel him. She glided her hips back and forth in an effort to feel his caress. And then, he did. His thumb brushed over the sensitive bundle of nerves and she cried out, desperate for more.

"Och, lass, ye're so passionate," he murmured. "So wet…"

He continued to tease her sex, stroking that hardened knot, sliding his fingers between the folds, and then he pushed one inside her. It was nearly her undoing. Shona was certain she'd never felt this much pleasure before. She could barely keep her eyes open. And her hands… What could she do with them? She wanted to touch him. To give him just as much pleasure.

She shifted down his length, gently stroking along the rippling muscles of his torso, tracing his old scars, and kissing them as she went.

"Lass—" he said through gritted teeth and tensing.

"Shh," she whispered, not wanting him to be self-conscious about his wounds. "Ye're beautiful, too."

"They dinna bother ye? The scars?" There was pain in his voice, as though he expected her to reject him.

Shona locked her gaze onto his and shook her head. "Nay, Ewan. We all have scars. Some are simply more visible than others."

His expression softened and he squinted as he studied her, a look of wonder in his eyes. "Where did ye come from?" he whispered.

The question made her uncomfortable, for if she truly thought about it, she couldn't remember. And did she want to? Was it worth dredging up a past that had kept itself hidden?

Growing braver, and hoping to make him forget, she trailed a finger beneath the blanket.

Both of them let out a moan when her fingers slid over the hardened length of him. His cock was satiny soft, and yet rock hard.

Ewan skimmed his hands over her back, exploring her spine, and leaning forward to kiss her neck. He glided over her collarbone and back down toward her breasts. When she touched the tip of his erection, Ewan groaned and bit her nipple, a mix of pleasure and pain shooting through her. That only urged her further. She wrapped her hand around his cock and squeezed. Her bold move earned her another nip of his teeth.

But that didn't stop her. Nay, she gripped him tight, moved her hand up and down, reveling in the hitch in his breath, the way his body trembled. A drop of moisture beaded the tip. She swiped it with her thumb then pressed her finger to her lips.

Ewan's gaze burned into hers, his jaw muscle clenched. "Where have ye been all my life, lass?"

He gripped her buttocks tight, and flipped her over, landing hard on top of her. The crash of his body, the weight of him tumbling her into the mattress, was an all-new and delicious sensation. His gaze caught hers, a wolfish grin on his delectable lips. She'd lost her grip on his cock, missing its weight in her hand. Ewan pinned her arms over her head and thrust his knees between her thighs, spreading them wide. Shona's mouth opened, a shocked gasp escaping as air hit her sensitive parts. She gulped. Swallowed hard. Pulsing skin, thrumming insides, Shona was desperate to feel him inside her.

"Ye'll hurt yourself," she admonished.

"Hush, lass, I'm perfectly well." He leaned down to nip her lower lip. "Keep your hands where they are."

Reaching between them, he parted her slippery folds, the head of his cock sliding deliciously along the seam. Shona wanted to grab hold of him, nearly did, but kept her hands above her head. Ewan groaned, notched his cock at her entrance and with a pivot of his hips, he drove inside her.

Shona stiffened, knowing that allowing this much was taking it too far, that she shouldn't let him continue… But the pleasure was intense. His thick cock stretched her, took charge of her body and she couldn't escape her startled cry of pleasure. Deep and shattering, she felt herself cave inside. Wanting desperately the connection he was giving her. The touch of another human, for a moment she could pretend that all was well, that she was happy, and that all her loneliness had faded away.

Ewan didn't move further, but kept himself buried deep inside her. He dipped his head and captured her lips, tugging at them with his teeth, sliding his tongue over the sting. Shona wrapped her legs up around his hips, wanted to flatten her hands to the part of his chest that was not injured, to feel his heart beat beneath her fingertips. He must have felt her hands twitch for he gave a wicked grin and tore a bit of linen from the bed sheet.

"May I?" he asked, sliding the length of fabric over her wrists.

Shona could barely breathe, excitement pulsed through her with such intensity. She nodded her consent, and whimpered with pleasure as he gently slid the fabric along her wrists, tying her to the headboard, all the while, his thick cock pulsing inside her. Her eyes closed as she tilted her hips and pleasure seared her insides.

"Look at me," he demanded. "I want to watch ye, watching me, as I pleasure ye."

Shona opened her eyes, and when their gazes connected, he moved. Slowly, he withdrew from her body, every disappearing inch making her want to shout in protest. She bit her lip, then cried out, her eyes slamming shut, as he thrust hard back inside.

"Open your eyes," he said softly. He ran a hand along one of her thighs, lifted it from around his hip to his shoulder, making his cock slide deeper inside her. "Do ye like this?"

Shona nodded, bit her lip, tried hard to keep her eyes from rolling into the back of her head in ecstasy.

"Tell me, lass. What do ye like?"

Zounds, he wanted her to speak? She wasn't sure she could. "I... I like when ye push inside me."

"Like this?" He pulled out, thrust back in, deeper this time, hitting a part of her that made her whimper with pleasure and pain.

She nodded.

Ewan repeated the move, trailing a kiss from her ankle to her calf as he did it. Slowly, he bent over her, until his chest was touching hers, and he captured her mouth for another fiery kiss. Hips pushing back and forth, cock driving deep then withdrawing, hands and mouth everywhere, Shona couldn't take the pleasure. Couldn't keep her eyes open. She shut them tight, gasped with every move he made. Tilted her hips in greedy anticipation every time he withdrew. Pleasure she'd never known built up inside her. Intense pressure. The need to break free. To explode. To scream. Her body wound tight, and she could barely control her movements, her breaths or the gasps and moans that escaped her.

Her warrior whispered naughty things in her ear, words of encouragement, told her how much he liked her tight cunt clutching his cock, how wet she was and how he wanted to devour every part of her. It was more than she could handle, and yet, everything she wanted.

Shona's body shattered. Gripped by an overpowering pulse within, her sex spasmed, trembling in torrents, and powerful, pleasure-filled sensation rushed over her like the storm that raged outside. She keened, bucked upward, her body bowing.

"Och, lass, that's it, let it come," Ewan encouraged, pounding hard into her, gripping tight to her buttocks. And then he too was groaning, shouting her name as he pulled from her body, gripped his cock and spilled his seed on her belly.

"To prevent..." he started to say, but trailed off as he leaned down to slide his tongue over her lips.

"I know," she said with a smile. "Thank ye."

Ewan gently untied her wrists, kissing the insides where her pulse beat. Shona watched him, trying not to stare with wonder, with excitement, with something else she dared not put a name to. He wiped her belly clean with the sheet, kissed her languidly and then collapsed to the side of her, an arm and leg dangling off the side of the bed.

Moments later, his soft even breaths sounded against Shona's ear. He'd fallen asleep. And then doubt wound its way inside her mind. Was their lovemaking only the result of her tincture? Or had it been as real and powerful to him as it had been to her?

CHAPTER NINE

EWAN dreamed of beautiful things.

He dreamed of a red-haired fairy dancing naked, her creamy skin glowing in the hearth light. He felt her kiss on his lips, on his scars. He felt the slide of her velvet warmth encasing his cock. But more than that, there was something special in the rocking of their bodies, in the intense stares as they gazed into each other's eyes.

Now that he'd dreamed it, now that he'd had it, he wanted it forever.

And while he might have thought that possible coming out of his foggy state, he knew that was *impossible*.

Whatever fantasies he'd allowed himself to believe while under the influence of her delicious scent, her touch — they were just that, illusions.

Ewan was a warrior. But not just any warrior. He was Captain of the Guard for Laird Logan Grant. He was second to the Guardian of Scotland, protector of the realm. Next to his laird, Ewan ensured the safety of the castle, the village, indeed all of Gealach lands and Scotland itself. He could not be bound to one woman.

Furthermore, what did he have to offer a woman? He had no past. No family. Only his duties.

And yet, Shona had shown him something that he'd not had with any other. Care — she'd taken *care* of him. He had no one. When he'd been injured before he'd been at the mercy of his laird, his laird's wife and their healers. They'd done well in tending him, but it wasn't the same.

A wife looked forward to a man's homecoming more so than his master and companions. More than Hildie and her lot. Shona had given him a taste of what wifely compassion could be. What having a woman at his side was like — someone to look after him, to care *about* him.

Then again, he wanted to be the one taking care of her, and so far she'd played nursemaid to him for several days and he'd done nothing for her. The past several days he'd seen in blurs. But making love to her — that was no blur. He could recall it vividly.

And he knew without a doubt it couldn't happen again. He had to get back to the castle. He had to leave this place, leave her. And never look back, because she made him want things he couldn't have, nor did he deserve.

He opened his eyes, no longer feeling the warmth of her body beside him as he had all night.

Indeed, she was not within the tiny cottage. Ewan took a moment to glance around the comfortable room. It was clean and well-maintained. How had she been able to do that without the help of a man? Who was he kidding? There *had* to be a man. A woman as beautiful as she would never survive in the woods alone.

Perhaps all his ruminations about why she couldn't be his were simply there to protect his pride. Because from the looks of things, she wasn't free to give herself to him, anyway.

Ewan threw back the blanket and sat up, a little dizzy and his body aching. His head pounded. She'd done a good job sewing him up.

He stood on shaky legs, taking a moment to let his weight settle on his limbs before he found his plaid. It was folded neatly on top of a chest at the foot of the bed — washed and dried. His belt was with it. He pleated the fabric and belted it around his hips. No shirt. Judging from the look of himself, the shirt had been destroyed. 'Haps if he looked inside the chest or the wardrobe he could borrow one of her husband's. Ewan frowned. He'd never wear another man's shirt —

especially not her man's. He slipped on his hose and boots, feeling more like himself already.

Och, what did it matter, he only intended to find her. To tell her thanks and to be on his way.

But first, he had to see what that heavenly scent was. A loud grumble in his belly implored him to investigate. He trudged toward the hearth and lifted the ladle full of stew to his lips and took a sip. Delicious. He took a few more sips. He'd have to tell her what an excellent cook she was when he thanked her for her nurturing.

Ewan opened the door, blinking wildly at the sun shining into his face. He held up his arm until his eyes adjusted. Then made his way toward the barn. Inside he found a few animals and a rough looking horse.

The horse nickered to him—the sound oddly familiar. Ewan looked closer, his eyes deceiving him. "What in bloody…?"

That was *his* horse. The poor animal's mane had been chopped off and he looked as though he'd been left out in a mud storm.

"What happened to ye, Bhaltair?"

The horse shook his head and blew out a disgusted sigh.

"At least ye look well fed," Ewan said, taking note of the oats in the bucket. "Very well fed."

How could she afford such fine oats?

The clues were slowly coming together. There was no doubt now. There was a man in her life already.

'Twas only a matter of time before the man returned. Exiting the barn, he caught sight of Shona on the opposite side, stacking wood she'd likely just cut. The top of an ax was buried inside a large flattened stump she must have been using to hold the smaller logs in place.

Wasn't that a man's job? Odd. But impressive.

Ewan quietly approached her, but she must have sensed his presence for she glanced up, concern in her eyes but a smile on her lips.

"Ye lied to me," he growled, surprised by the vehemence and emotion laced in his own voice.

She glanced toward the barn, a frown on her lips and when she glanced back at him, he swore there was regret in her eyes. "About your horse? I had to cut his mane, I apologize, but it was for your safety."

Ewan slowly shook his head. "Not about that— though I'm not sure whether to be offended or not."

"I have lied to ye about nothing else," she said, shifting her gaze.

Ewan stepped closer. Shona didn't retreat, she straightened, her feet firmly planted in the ground. The way her breath heaved from the strain of her work pushed her breasts against the gown in an enticing way. He could see the outline of her perfectly round bosom, and the closer he got, the tighter her nipples grew. Instantly, his body reacted, cock growing hard and desire whipping through him.

Ewan stopped walking. He couldn't desire her. Not when he'd found out she had someone. Yet, he did. Fiercely.

"Where is he?" he demanded.

She swallowed hard. "Who?"

"Dinna lie to me again, Shona."

She squared her shoulders and stared him straight in the face, confusion marring her features. "I didna lie to ye."

Anger sliced through him. Ewan closed the gap between them and gripped her shoulders. He brought his face within an inch of hers, trying to ward off the intense need to kiss her, to crush her delicious body to his and claim ownership. She was warm to his touch and a soft sheen of perspiration shone on her skin. He wanted to lick every inch of her clean, bury himself ballocks deep inside her until they both cried out. The intensity of his need was startling and disturbing.

"Ye'll hurt yourself. Ye must go back inside and rest," she said softly.

"Tell me," he growled.

Her little pink tongue flicked out to swipe over her lips. Ballocks but she was entirely too enticing for her own good.

"Tell ye what?" Her gaze searched his face, looking for answers.

"Tell me…" But did he really want to hear that she had a man? That a husband had already claimed her? That all the things he'd fantasized about her being *his* woman—no matter how illogical and unrealistic they were—could never be?

"Let me take ye back inside," she soothed, reaching up to place her hands over his and squeezing. Just the same way she'd squeezed his cock.

Her fingers were warm, but what got him the most was the shot of desire that sparked in her eyes. His cock pulsed, hard with untamed need.

And he didn't care at that moment if she had a man or three. Ewan tugged her against him, ignoring the ache to his wounds and brushed his mouth over hers. He wanted to devour her, delve inside her mouth and never leave, but he didn't want to frighten her away. Didn't want her to deny him.

But he need not have worried. Shona slid her tongue out to taste the line of his lips, thrusting inside his mouth to kiss him with abandon. A soft moan escaped her, and she lifted on her tiptoes, the crux of her thighs cradling his rigid length. Heat cupped his arousal, showing him she, too, was filled with need for him.

Ewan wanted to pleasure her and punish her all at the same time. Without realizing it—or maybe she did—Shona embodied everything he wanted and couldn't have. He wanted to take her. He wanted to touch her, to hear her cry out, to quiver around him. Ewan had always been cautious, taking only what he was offered. Ever since he was a lad and Logan had saved him. He remembered little of his childhood, but what he did know was that he was loyal to a fault.

Well, this time, he was going to take what wasn't his, and he was damned well going to enjoy it.

He gripped her hips and lifted her into the air, hands sliding down her thighs and forcing them around his hips. Shona moaned into his mouth, her hands wrapping around his neck as she held tight to him. Primal heat ripped through him. She wanted him — and she shouldn't.

Ewan took the five or so steps toward the barn wall and pressed her back up against it, rocking his body against hers so she could feel his rigid cock pressing into her.

"I want ye," he murmured.

He tore his mouth from hers and skimmed his teeth down her neck to the top of her gown.

"I need ye," she answered, yanking down the fabric, freeing a single breast to his view and he gladly tugged the turgid peak into his mouth.

Grinding her up against the wall with his hips, he made quick work of pushing her gown up her thighs until he felt the wet heat of her cunt against his palm.

He sucked harder on her nipple, reveling in the tiny gasps and moans slipping from her lips. With a flick of his wrist, his belt was undone and his plaid pooling at his feet. He gripped his cock, slid it through her wet folds and then surged forward.

Shona's head fell back against the barn wall and a moan tore from her throat.

"Ye like it hard?" he asked, pounding into her. "Do ye like it when I take ye like this?"

Her fingernails sunk into the flesh at his shoulders, her feet hooked at the small his back.

"Aye," she crooned.

If she was going to lie to him, to pretend she wasn't already taken, then he was going to take his pleasure as she gave it. Base and full of feral heat. He almost felt sorry for the sot she was linked to, for Shona was minx and a half.

"Harder," she moaned, her hips swiveling rapidly. "Oh, Ewan."

At least she'd gotten his name right. And he was going to give her exactly what she asked for.

Bracing his feet, and holding tight to her hips, he drove deep and hard inside her. He was relentless, pushing her against the wood, slamming his cock in and out. The sound of their flesh smacking echoed in the small yard, but he didn't care. He hoped her man came home and found them like this.

Ewan's mouth crashed onto hers, swallowing her cries as he thrust harder and faster still. And then her grip on his shoulders tightened, her body stiffened, and her slick, tight cunt quivered and squeezed. A moan deep in her throat pushed past their kiss as she climaxed—enough to make him burst inside, too. He sank in deep as spasms caught him, then recalled she wasn't his and pulled out at the last second, the rest of his seed spilling to the ground.

Fucking her would have been a lot more satisfying if he'd been able to spend inside her all the way. Ballocks, but he should have done it anyway. Should have truly claimed her, husband be damned.

Ewan set her down and staggered backward, naked both physically and emotionally.

Shona ran her hand through her hair, her hands visibly shaking.

"That was…" she started and stopped. Stooping to pick up his plaid and belt she came forward to hand it to him.

Too wrecked from what had just happened and the thoughts that wrenched though his mind, he grabbed the items and backed away from her, shaking his head. He turned his back on her and headed for the cottage.

WHAT the bloody hell?

Shona stared at Ewan's retreating figure, pain ripping through her chest. How could he just walk away from her in such disgust? What had she done wrong? He'd seemed to enjoy their lovemaking—even when she'd made a wanton demand for him to thrust harder.

Glowering at his back, she refused to let him treat her like that. She marched forward, intent on telling him exactly how she felt. Inside the cottage, he'd re-pleated his plaid and was belting it at his hips. Her healer's eye took in the bandages, pleased not to see any blood on the surface.

"Why did ye walk away from me?" She tried to keep the hurt from her voice.

Ewan swiped a hand over his face and shook his head again refusing to answer.

The stubborn mule.

"Why won't ye answer me?" Her voice came out soft and confused. It wouldn't do to show how angry his reaction had made her, how much it hurt, too.

"I've no right to ye, lass, and no place in being cross, but I am all the same."

"Cross? Why should ye be angry?" She turned to glance out the door at the spot where they'd unleashed their passion. "What we did was… a sin, aye, but not unnatural."

He gaped at her with exasperation that made her take a step back. The muscle in his jaw was clenched tight. He blew out a breath and shook his head again. "'Tis no matter. This was a mistake."

Shona felt anger bubbling in her belly, hands coming to her hips, she stared hard at the warrior before her. "What was a mistake? Me saving your life or you touching me?"

He shrugged. "Maybe both. Ye should have left me."

What felt like a fist socking her in the stomach took Shona's breath away. A mistake. Since the moment she'd seen him fighting, this man had captivated her. She'd risked her life taking him back to her cottage.

Had saved his life. Had laid her soul open and let him make love to her not once, but twice, and he claimed it was all a mistake?

Her mouth fell open in shock. The fever must still hold him captive despite him being able to walk around—and hold her up against a wall. That could be the only reason behind his odd behavior. Unless...

"I dinna believe ye." Her words came out strong, funneling the anger that burned in her chest.

"What?" Ewan whipped around, torment crinkling the corners of his eyes and drawing his mouth down.

She took a step closer to him, and locked her eyes on his, seeing their pain-filled depths, and wishing he'd tell her what had him so shaken up.

Shona straightened, braced for his anger. "Ye're the one lying now."

CHAPTER TEN

EWAN gaped at the fiery lass who stood before him. Never in his life had so many conflicting emotions wrapped their way around him inside, tugging, splitting, nothing catching hold and nothing making sense.

"Just what in bloody hell do ye think I'm lying about? I'm not the one traipsing about seducing wounded men." The moment the words left his mouth he wished to tug them back. To suck them in like a wind tunnel sucked a galleon into the ocean's cold, dark depths. But it was too late.

Across from him, Shona's face crumbled into a tumult of reactions that he himself felt deep in his chest.

Anger. Sadness. Grief. Her hand flashed out and she struck him hard across the face.

And he let her. He could have stopped her, but he didn't. He needed that slap. Needed to feel the sting of her anger. Relished the burn on his face.

"How dare ye speak to me like that!"

He advanced toward her in a single long step, both their chests heaving with passion. "And why shouldn't I? 'Tis what happened, is it not? Tell me, how many men have ye brought back to your little croft? How many have you fed with your tinctures and then lain with?"

He watched her grind her teeth, an angry spark flashing in her eyes. When she raised her hand to slap him this time, he gripped her wrist, stopping her in mid-air. Her pulse beat hard beneath his fingertips and Ewan couldn't help it, he couldn't stop himself. His anger and desire exploded and he caught her chin, crushing his mouth against hers. He kissed her in a hard, possessive, bruising kiss. She bit his lip savagely, hotly. And when she opened her mouth allowing him to plunder deep inside, he tasted his blood on her tongue.

Ewan seized her tight, her lush body pressed to his solid one and his cock, full and hard with need, ground against her belly. He wanted to pound inside her, to thrust away the pain and anger that swelled in his heart.

Gripping her hand, he pulled her palm to his rigid shaft. "Do ye feel that? Ye do this to me. No other has possessed me as ye do."

Shona glared up at him. If she'd had arrows for eyes he'd be as dead as the man she felled in the forest. She struggled against him, and when he wouldn't let her go she grasped his cock tight enough to be both sensual and cause a little pain.

"Is this what ye want, Ewan?"

God, it was what he wanted and so much more. But not like this. He hissed a breath. "I dinna want to be second."

"Who said ye are? There's no one else here."

"Not yet."

Shona shook her head. "Ye're a bastard."

He was, and he was coming apart in her hand because she still held his cock and was slowly stroking upward.

"I dinna want ye to stop, yet I want ye to." He wrapped his arms around the small of her back and squeezed her buttocks, tugging her closer.

"That makes no sense."

"Nothing makes sense to me, anymore." Especially this. The attraction he had for her went beyond sanity and reason. He was drowning in it. "I have to have ye. Have to taste ye."

Ewan swept her up in his arms and carried her to the small bed.

"We shouldn't. Not again," she said, trembling beneath him. One look in her eyes told him she didn't tremble from fear though, but from the need he, too, felt inside.

"I canna help it." Ewan covered her with his body. "Ye've sucked away the last traces of my control."

And sucking... The thought of her mouth... Would he never be rid of such thoughts? Shona licked her lips. Blast, could he even ask?

"I want..." he started, then closed his eyes. With Hildie and her crew it was easy to make demands. But with Shona...

"Tell me what ye want." A potent hunger filled her voice.

But Ewan couldn't ask something he wasn't sure she was willing to give, and so he yanked up her gown, and stared down at the fiery curls and the pink petals of her cunny that shone damp.

"I want to taste ye." He ran a single finger through the slick folds and watching her tense and eyes widen.

"What?"

"Has no man ever run his tongue over your mons?"

Shona licked her lips and shook her head. Interest and hunger sparked in her eyes. "I didna know..."

"I'm going to lick ye clean, lass."

Her lips parted, a soft moan escaping, and his cock jumped with the need to fill that warm, velvet cavern. To have her tongue run over his cock. She must have seen a visceral reaction in his eyes for she glanced down at his groin and licked her lips again.

"Can I... can we...?" she asked.

Ewan grinned. "If ye're saying what I think ye are, then I'd be verra happy to oblige ye, lass."

"Show me."

"Get undressed." Ewan stood from the bed, loosened his belt and let his plaid fall to the floor. He kicked off his boot and tore off his hose.

Shona stared at his solid shaft, seemingly immobilized by the sight. Ewan held out his hand to her and pulled her to stand. One more moment of abandon and then he'd be on his way. This was too much for him. He lay on the bed, watching her strip down to her slick smooth skin.

When she was naked, he beckoned her closer. "Ye're going straddle my face, but facing my toes. This way we can both put our tongues to the other."

Her eyes widened, but her lips quirked into a seductive smile.

"Sinful," she whispered.

"Completely." He flashed her a wicked grin and a wink. "Now, come here."

He grabbed her hand and tugged her forward.

Ewan positioned her so that her thighs were on either side of his face, and he ran his hands over her round rump, breathing in her delicious musky scent.

Shona leaned down on her elbows, her breath washing over his cock. He shuddered, and barely had time to breathe when she took his shaft into her mouth. Her tongue swirled over his sensitive skin. She sucked soft and slow, then hard and fast.

"*Mo chreach*, lass, where did ye learn..." But he didn't finish his question, because he didn't want to know the answer. It only reminded him of the argument they'd never finished.

Her fingers wrapped around him working him up and down in rhythm with her mouth. Time for him to reciprocate. Holding onto her thighs, he leaned up and flicked his tongue over the pink pearl she'd exposed to him. Shona jerked and moaned, the sound vibrating over his skin. If she kept up this pace he would burst before he had a chance to make her climax.

That wouldn't do.

Ewan wanted this last time together to be explosive and pleasurable for them both. A punishing memory.

With his tongue flattened, he licked her from one end to the other, stroking over her folds and the tiny knot of nerves. He dipped a finger, then two, inside her, stroking over the slick velvet walls until he found the pressure point that made her cry out. He was relentless in his pursuit of her satisfaction, alternately stroking her soft flesh with his tongue and sucking, and plunging fast then slow with his fingers.

Shona rocked her hips back and forth, her mouth picking up speed around his cock as her enjoyment increased. Her moans were soft then louder and came faster together, until finally she cried out, her cunny walls tightening and spasming around his fingers. Ewan thrust his hips hard, and she took all of him in, sucking harder as she climaxed, causing him to let go, a powerful release gripping him.

Ewan growled his pleasure, "Fuck, lass."

She collapsed on top of him, then realized what she'd done and murmured apologies as she slipped to the side.

Ewan swiped his hand over his face, the intoxicating scent of her everywhere. He stood from the bed and used her water bowl to splash his face.

His blood ran both hot and cold as he stared at her lush body on the bed. Immediately he wanted her again. Wanted to possess her. Wanted her to wrap herself around him and never let go.

Impossible.

"I have to leave. Now."

Shona sat up, staring at him with a blank expression. Her eyes were shuttered, closing off her feelings from him. He didn't know if that was because she was relieved to see him go or because it pained her. And it shouldn't be his concern.

Shona dressed, not meeting his gaze as she did so. He pleated his plaid in record time.

"Have ye never had anything good in your life, Ewan?" Her voice was soft as she asked it, though he could tell by the tremble in her tone that she was affected a lot more by what had transpired than she was willing to admit. "Is it all pain and suffering? Must ye push your darkness into all things light?"

This time she did meet his gaze and the pain he saw there nearly tore his heart from his chest. Likewise, her words took him aback, hitting a chord inside that he'd rather leave untouched. Aye, his life had been filled with pain. It had been filled with darkness. Light wasn't a part of it. He was a warrior. No family. No ties to anyone other than his laird. He owed a duty to his clan. That was it. A woman would only complicate things — and a woman not free to be his would bring on a world of suffering he wasn't willing to explore.

He had to put some distance between them. Had to sort things out in his mind.

She stood before him, shoulders squared, waiting for his response, but he didn't even know how to reply. So he remained silent, lips clamped closed when all he really wanted to do was tug her back into his arms, to feel her warmth wrap around him again.

"I can barely remember beyond the last five years. And what memories I can dredge up are nothing but desolate sadness." She pressed her fist to her chest. "And it hurts, deep inside. Dinna take away from me the few moments of pleasure ye've given. Dinna ye dare!"

Her admission only fueled his anger. How dare she try to tell him that he'd given her the only bit of happiness she'd known. What did she take him for? A complete fool? "Save your paltry confessions for your husband."

The lass took a step back, stunned. Her expression could have been the same if he'd slapped her.

"My husband?"

"Aye—I know about him."

"But, I—"

He cut her off before she could try to manipulate him further. "Dinna say it. Now, if ye'll kindly point me in the direction of my weapons I'll be on my way."

Tears sparked in Shona's eyes, but he forced himself not to look at her, not to see what was shining there. The emotions running rampant in his own mind were too much to handle, he couldn't deal with hers, as well. It was all too much.

"Ye're a fool, Ewan."

Resentment flooded him—most of it aimed at himself. He hardened his expression. "I agree. Where are my things?"

Shona pressed her lips together until they were white, studying him hard. She looked as though she wanted to say something to him, but thought better of it. Disappointment she didn't try to hide flared in her gaze. "They are in the chest." Her voice cracked and she took a deep breath. "I'll ready your horse."

"I'll ready my own damn horse." The anger surging through Ewan was unrelenting, and he felt horrible inside with each word he uttered. He was being monstrous to her. She didn't deserve it, no matter how much she'd lied to him.

His anger was all his own doing. More irritation at what he'd let himself believe than at her for her own actions. Who was he to say what she did or didn't do? And what did it matter? Married women had been known to take lovers. She was no different.

And yet, he'd wanted to think she was. But most of all, he'd wanted to believe she was alone. Free to be with him.

Unable to look at her as a large tear spilled down her cheek, Ewan marched toward the chest, determined not to stare at the bed where they'd shared a magical moment the night before. He wrenched open the carved lid, half fearing what he'd see inside—another man's things.

But there were no other man's things. He refused to think of the implications of that as he sifted through a few linens to find his weapons, minus his dagger. 'Haps he'd lost it during his battle with the bloody MacDonalds.

Ballocks, but he'd wasted too much time here already. He didn't even know how many of his men had made it through the woods, and if Flynn had ever been found. Logan would have likely gone back out to look for him, and he'd never forgive himself if his laird was hurt.

Blast it all, but he had her to thank that he was even still alive. If she'd not killed the one bastard with her bow and warned him about the horse, he'd have been more seriously injured—probably killed.

And he was a real bastard for not at least thanking her. For taking advantage of her sweet, passionate nature. No matter how bruised his ego, she deserved his gratitude.

Ewan turned around to apologize to Shona, but he was alone. The door stood slightly ajar as though she'd just slipped out. He was at the door in two steps, yanking it open. But she was not visible outside, either. She'd probably ignored him — as she should have — and had gone into the barn to help him with Bhaltair. His gut twisted, making him feel sick.

Why had he lashed out at her when she'd been nothing but be kind to him? Share herself with him. Opened up to him. Looking back, either she was a very good liar, or she'd shown him her true self.

Was it jealousy, perhaps, that made him act the way he did?

He'd begged her to make love to him the first, second and third time. He'd barely given her a choice, even if she had encouraged him with her sexy whimpers and heated body.

This was his fault.

He was an arse.

Ewan made his way across the lawn to the barn, but when he stepped inside, she wasn't there, either. Bhaltair greeted him with a nicker, but the pig and goat seemed to stare at him accusingly, as if they'd already heard of his crude behavior.

Hands on his hips, Ewan looked around the barn, puzzled. Where could she have gone?

Back out in the clearing before her little cottage, he called out to her. "Shona!"

But there was no reply, and a quick walk around the cottage did not turn her up, either. She'd simply disappeared.

And he didn't blame her.

"Shona, come back to me! I need to speak with ye."

The lone bleating goat from the barn answered him.

"I'm sorry," he called out. "Forgive me, lass. Please come out."

But the only answers were the whisper of the wind against his cheek, and Bhaltair's annoyed whinnying from his stall.

Served him right for acting like a first-rate bastard.

"I..." What? What could he say? Confess that he'd only ever been selfish when it came to the lasses and that she'd finally opened his eyes to what it could be like if he weren't such an arse? Ewan shook his head.

"Ye should nay be out here all alone," he called again. "There are many dangerous beasts in these woods."

But she'd seemed to disappear into thin air—or at least she was doing a damn good job of ignoring him. And aye, there were dangerous beasts, one of which was he.

With a frown on his face, and his mood blacker than a raging storm, he returned to the barn to ready his horse. With one last fruitless search around the cottage for Shona, he took off toward where he thought he might find the road to Castle Gealach.

FROM her haven in the trees, Shona watched Ewan ride away.

She swiped away the tears tracking down her cheeks.

"Strength," she whispered.

Strength was what had gotten her as far as she was, and strength was what would keep her going.

All the painful words he said still bounced around inside her skull, ratcheting off her bones. But she pushed them aside, wiping her mind clean just as she wiped at her face. Ewan was not the man she thought he was. Whatever she'd thought him to be was a figment of her imagination. She'd been dreaming of something she'd wanted for so long, and it just so happened that she'd pushed that dream onto him. From his flowery words, his whispered sentiments when they'd made love the first time, she'd thought it was something he wanted, too. But he wouldn't admit that he was lying to himself, to her.

Only that he wanted no part.

And who was she to make a man love her? To make a man want her?

Had she forced him somehow to make love to her? To cherish her and worship her body? To give her pleasure? Mayhap she was the witch they'd all accused her of being.

The man had been clear that he wanted to part with her, and still she'd kissed him and let him touch her until she cried out. And what she'd done to him in turn... it had been explosive.

Yet, he'd shown his loathing at what they'd done.

Except, now he had looked contrite. He had come looking for her. He had asked for her forgiveness. Well, she'd let him trick her once, she couldn't allow it to happen again. Though, could she truly say he'd tricked her? It was her own fault. She'd wanted him, desired him. Had practically thrown herself on top of him when she should have been taking care of him.

Well, 'haps she'd taken care of him in more ways than one.

Nay, nay! Shona refused to let herself think that way, to let herself be the one to ruin such wonderful memories. No regrets. That was how she had to feel about it, because deep down, she didn't regret it. She treasured it. Those brief moments when he'd held her in his arms had been magical. Beautiful. Shattering.

Mayhap that was the saddest part of all—that she'd let herself be swept up by him and the emotions he elicited. She'd fallen hard for a fantasy that would never be a reality.

As soon as the sound of Bhaltair's hoof beats no longer echoed on the wind, she climbed from her perch and smoothed her skirts.

A flash of memory took her breath, and she found herself falling against the tree, her hand pressed over her heart. The woman in the vision was practically a stranger. Did not look like her, did not speak like her, did not dress like her. Nothing like her at all, except she knew in the bottom of her heart—it was *her*. This stranger who wore bizarre clothes and spoke oddly and smiled at a man who passed her by without a second glance—that was her. She stood among buildings taller than a castle and made from a material other than stone. The roads were paved with a seemingly endless black stone. Fast-moving, loud objects whipped past her, making her dizzy.

But where could the memory have come from?

The tears started anew and she sank to the ground filled with sorrow and confusion. The past several years she'd felt like she had to relearn so much. Like a bairn just born, but a woman grown, and she didn't know why. She would be forever grateful to Rory for finding her and protecting her some five years before. Without him, she'd likely have died of starvation or been rounded up by one of the savages who brutally harmed Ewan.

When Rory had found her cowering behind a tree, dirt-stained and crying, the only thing she'd known was her name. He'd smiled down at her, held out his hand and offered to help. Had told her that the land around Gealach had a tendency to draw various wary people to them and that he had once been in her shoes.

Before now, she'd never thought about what he meant when he'd said it, other than he'd been down on his luck. Now, she wondered if he, too, had memories of another time and place where he looked like a stranger to himself.

Is that what happened to Rory? Had he returned to wherever it was he was from? Had he decided she was able to fend for herself?

Shona gazed up at the bits of sky that were visible through the branches of the tree she leaned against. All the grayness of the storms had disappeared and blue peeked between the leaves. At least Ewan would have a decent ride back to wherever he was headed.

With a soft sob escaping her throat, she crawled to a stand, her shoulders slouched with the heaviness of her heart. But she had to move on, had warned herself that this would happen with Ewan.

Even that stranger who sometimes sent her memories, she could not recall had been destined to be alone. This was what Fate had in store for her—no matter the lifetime.

She trudged back to the cottage, finding it as dark and gloomy as her mood. Ewan's scent lingered. So did the words he'd whispered to her. They floated in the air like ghosts, haunting her. Too tired to eat her stew, Shona barred the door and then collapsed on her bed. She curled up with the pillow and blanket Ewan had used, breathing in the scent of him, the scent of their lovemaking and pretending that he lay behind her, cradling her.

Awareness of her loneliness had been on the forefront of her mind for two years at least. Even when

Rory had been here with her, she'd never truly been his. He'd never opened up to her, even when she tried. His heart had always belonged to another, and to him she'd always been a long lost sister returned.

But it wasn't until now that she realized she could drift away and no one would be the wiser. That she'd not made any memories in this new life that she could share with anyone. Except Ewan. And he'd thrust her aside, accused her of being a harlot.

The stark truth of the matter was that if anyone had lied, it was she. Shona had lied to herself.

Was *still* lying to herself.

Because even now, she wanted Ewan with a stunning desperation. Still wanted everything he'd not been willing to offer her. Wanted to run toward the road and call out for him to return to her. To beg him to… what? She couldn't change his mind. She couldn't make him love her, or even want her.

And sadly, she'd likely never see him again.

CHAPTER ELEVEN

THE ride to Castle Gealach was painful.

Aye, Ewan's injuries throbbed with a dull ache, but what hurt the most was unexplainable. A part of him, deep inside, stung with regret.

For the seventh time, he pulled Bhaltair to a stop and turned around, though he didn't urge his horse forward. Muttering a curse, he clenched his jaw tight. Inside, his conscience warred with the need to return to his laird, ensuring that his men were all accounted for, and the intense need to return to Shona. To make sure she knew he was sorry for the words he'd said. To thank her for saving him. To tell her that the moments they'd shared had meant more to him than a simple few moments of fucking. That he didn't want to take away the pleasure he'd given her and that if he could he would have given her more.

The feelings cascading through him were wholly new — and goddamned irritating.

Life was so much easier when he didn't have to worry about anyone's feelings. When he went about his duties protecting Gealach, training the men and having Logan's back. That came naturally to him. He was an instinctive protector. Had been from the moment he could remember — up until meeting Shona.

Ewan had come to Gealach as a lad. Just when Logan had lost his parents and learned his deepest, darkest secret — that he was, in fact, the fraternal twin brother to the late King James. That the throne was his as he was born first. A secret and a burden that Logan didn't want any part of. Arriving half-starved and beaten, Ewan had needed a familiar face and a friend. Logan had needed a trustworthy confidant. Each was able to provide the other with what they needed. They'd been close ever since.

That made Ewan's decision to return to Gealach all the more clear. He owed Logan at least the knowledge that he was alive and well. Once he talked with his laird, he'd return to the woods — to Shona. He'd beg her forgiveness. Maybe even beg her to leave the husband she so obviously didn't love. Would ask her to take a chance on him...

Once more, Ewan turned his horse in the direction of the castle and took off at high speed. After several days cooped up in a barn, his mount was more than happy to keep the active pace. The road was clear of MacDonalds, and Ewan didn't know whether to be pleased or wary of that fact.

When he at last broke through the trees and rode out onto the moors, Castle Gealach loomed in the distance. From where he sat, all appeared well. The summer storms had ceased and all the grass and flowers upon the rolling landscape bloomed. A sheen of sweat covered his skin and Bhaltair was also slick from the exertion of their ride.

If he'd not been battling the MacDonalds and the Butcher the last several weeks, he might have thought he'd landed in paradise. That all was well with the world.

Lord, he prayed it would be soon. All he had to do was tell Logan about Shona. Confess that he may have found the one person who could complete him. Then defeat the MacDonalds and the Butcher. Feats that seemed a lot easier thought up than accomplished.

An image of Shona's sparkling eyes and sweet smile flashed in his mind. He missed her already. The thought struck him somewhere deep in his chest, bringing back that dull ache he'd felt upon leaving. He very nearly turned around again, but this close to the castle, one of the lookouts was bound to have seen him.

As Ewan got closer to the gate, arrows began to fly from the battlements landing around the ground where he rode.

"*Sguir!*" he ordered Bhaltair, who immediately ceased running and stood rigidly still.

Ewan held up his hand and waved to the men atop the ramparts.

"Cease your fire! 'Tis Ewan Fraser!" he called, not sure if at this distance they would even hear him.

With the hack job and mud that Shona had used to hide Bhaltair's identity, the men on the wall wouldn't recognize his horse. Bandaged up and missing a shirt, he didn't look exactly look himself, either.

An unintelligible shout sounded on the wind. Ewan could not tell if it was friendly or not and judging from the arrows piercing the ground at his horse's feet, he wasn't going to risk moving forward. Instead, he waved the strip of fabric he'd tossed over his shoulder in the air, hoping they'd take note it was Grant colors.

There was another shout he couldn't decipher and then the portcullis was drawn up and the gates opened. Four warriors rode out toward him at breakneck speed. Ewan kept his hands in the air. As the men closed in on him, they seemed to recognize him — in fact, Master of the Gate, Taig shouted out.

"Ewan! Ye bastard, we thought ye were dead."

Ewan grinned and flung his plaid back over his shoulder. "Alive and well, man."

The four stopped just in front of him. "Ye look like shite. Took a beating, did ye?" Taig's eyes roved over Ewan's injuries, a frown marring his features.

"Better than the bastards who inflicted the wounds," Ewan boasted.

"Where have ye been?" Taig asked.

"Saved by an angel." Ewan couldn't help but smile. "Well, not exactly. A fiery-haired lass who nursed me back to health."

The men raised their brows, but Taig nodded grimly. "Ye met *her*."

"Who?" Ewan's brow drew together and a vicious pang of jealousy stabbed him in the gut. If Taig had lain one finger on her, he would crush him right then and there.

"The Witch of the Wood."

Ewan narrowed his eyes, he somewhat remembered her saying that people thought her a witch. "She's no witch."

The men's eyes drew together, and they stared at him like he might have turned into a toad, or something worse.

"Best get ye inside, then," Taig said. "The laird will want to speak with ye."

"Aye, let us go." Ewan urged his horse forward and the men fell in beside him.

"Damned glad ye're back and that ye're not dead," Taig said. "We found Flynn, the poor lad nearly bled to death, but he's fine now."

"And the others?" Ewan asked.

"We lost one—Donald—but the others only took a few wounds."

"Were the MacDonalds captured?"

"Four of them. We took care of at least a dozen. The rest escaped, and we've not seen them about, yet."

"The Butcher?"

"Escaped."

Ewan nodded. Logan had probably already questioned the captives, but Ewan wanted to speak with them, too. They had to find The Butcher before he attacked again, else another innocent life be taken.

Bloody hell, the bastard better not go near Shona before Ewan had a chance to return to her. He'd rip the man limb from rotten limb. And he'd forever regret not turning around when he should have.

They passed through the gates of Gealach and excited shouts surrounded Ewan as people ran forward to welcome him home.

He smiled and dismounted, waving aside their excitement. There was no time for idle chatter. Making his way through the throng of people he headed for the castle, but before he could reach it, Logan and his wife Emma burst through the doors.

Tears brimmed in Emma's eyes and she smiled brightly up at him. "You're back," she said in her Sassenach accent.

"Aye." Ewan and Emma had formed a bond of friendship over the past year, and he cared for her as much as he would his own sister—if he had one.

"Where the bloody hell have ye been?" Logan growled, though a smile etched the sides of his lips.

"Saved by an angel," Ewan said, ignoring the grunts from the men beside him who believed Shona to be a witch. "And I want to return to the woods for her, but first, we have a lot to discuss."

A scowl covered Logan's face. "Aye. Best we get to my library."

"Do you want me to have a bath sent to your chamber?" Emma asked.

"My thanks, my lady, for thinking of me, but there's no time," Ewan said.

Emma frowned, her eyes roving over his form. "Food then? And the healer?"

Logan answered before Ewan had a chance. "Aye. Send the food to my library and the healer can check his wounds when we're done."

"Again my gratitude, my lady," Ewan said with a slight bow of his head.

Emma grinned and then sailed away, all elegance and beautiful perfection. The lass had arrived at Gealach timid and unsure of herself, but she'd blossomed under Logan's care. Furthermore, she'd lessened the brooding warrior within Logan and helped him to become an even greater man.

"How bad are your wounds?" Logan asked as they ascended the circular stair toward the laird's library.

"Not so bad. They weren't that deep. Got a massive knot on my head from a horse, but other than that, I'll live."

"Have a care the stitches do not reopen."

Ewan nodded, knowing Logan spoke directly about the last time he'd been stitched up and insisted he was well enough to walk about only to end up with a needle sewing him up again.

When they entered the library, Logan marched toward a chest, wrenched it open and threw a shirt at Ewan. "I love ye like a brother, man, but I dinna want to see ye half-naked while we discuss what happened."

Ewan chuckled. "And here I thought to entice ye."

Logan rolled his eyes. "A dram?"

"Och, aye. How about two?"

His laird poured two drams of whisky and handed him one. "Damned glad ye're back."

"Aye… Me, too." Ewan knocked back the burning liquid and passed his cup back for more.

Logan raised a skeptical brow as he poured him a second. "Why do ye not sound convinced?"

Ewan gripped the cup tight in his fist and frowned. "I shouldn't have left her."

"Who?"

"Shona."

Logan poured another dram and offered some to Ewan. They both drank, then sat down at the large map table.

"Who is Shona?"

Ewan tilted his head from side to side, cracking his neck. How to answer this question? "She is the one who saved me."

Logan grinned. "Didna know that the mighty Ewan would need saving by a lass."

"Och, but I did." In more ways than he was willing to admit. Guilt riddled his gut. How could he have been so blind? So stupid?

"Tell me what happened," Logan said.

Ewan relayed the events in the woods, and how Shona had brought him back to her cottage and treated his wounds. He told how he'd connected with her — leaving out that they'd made love. Instead, he played up the fact that she'd saved his life and now he owed her a favor in return.

"I have to go back for her," Ewan said. "I shouldn't have left her there. Not with the Butcher still running loose. And though there was evidence of a husband, he was not there the three days I was. She's alone out there, unprotected."

Logan shook his head. "If she has a husband, he'll not be pleased with your interference."

"Even if it's because an outlaw is ravaging the land? We could claim she sought refuge at the castle."

Logan drummed his fingers on the table. "That could work, but I fear she'll not be welcomed here by the people."

"Why not?"

"They think her a witch. The Witch of the Wood, they call her."

Ewan sat forward, slamming his fist on the table. "She's no witch!"

Logan grinned. "But she seems to have cast a mighty spell on ye."

"'Tis not like that. I... care for her wellbeing. I owe her that much."

"There is more. From what I've heard, she resides with a known outlaw—mayhap this is her husband."

As if the Butcher wasn't bad enough, now Ewan had to worry over a man she'd given herself to in holy matrimony? Though she did not appear abused by her husband, every day beyond she was connected to him put her life in danger. "She's wedded to an outlaw?"

Logan nodded. "Our own healers go to her for herbal remedies and knowledge. Man's name is Rory MacLeod. Cast out by his chief, but I dinna know why. Only got a warning from the MacLeod to look out for him. There's a price on his head. Might even have been the lass our village healer sent for when ye were attacked by Isabella MacDonald. She's well-respected among that group, but I fear what bringing her here will do."

Ewan still couldn't wrap his head around the fact that Shona was in imminent danger and he wasn't there to protect her.

"I have to go back. Now."

Logan stood, bracing his arms on the table as he stared at him. "Nay, Ewan. Ye canna. We need ye here. What has gotten into ye? The lass is not your concern."

Ewan gritted his teeth. The hell she wasn't! But what could he say to his laird? Whatever his answer was would merely sound crazy. He'd known the lass only a few days, but in that time he'd fallen hard. And that was as much as he was willing to admit.

"I'll not forsake the woman who saved my life. She shot a MacDonald, dragged my bleeding arse onto a horse and sewed me up. Without her, I'd be dead. To leave her unprotected goes against everything I believe in."

Logan ran a hand through his hair and then poured himself another generous portion of whisky. He didn't speak until he'd had two more drams, and then he said, "All right. Ye can go and get her. I'll speak with the clan. They will welcome her as an additional healer, or they will keep their opinions to themselves."

Relief flooded Ewan. "Much gratitude, my laird."

Logan nodded. "'Tis the least I can do after how many times ye've saved my arse. Now, shall we discuss the MacDonalds currently residing in the dungeon?"

"Aye. What have they to say?"

"The Butcher has orders from Chief MacDonald, we know that much. But we know not what the orders are, beyond plundering, pillaging and raping. Also from what the MacDonald lads have let slip, there are more coming. Another war is imminent."

Ewan shook his head. "When will the bastard learn his lesson?"

"Apparently not until he's met the end of my sword."

"So it has come to that?" The clan had been ravaged by war for years now. The last several months they'd seen peace, had been able to heal and grow, but now they'd be forced to face the danger of battle again. They were a strong clan though, and strong clans survived.

"Aye. The Earl of Arran will be displeased that the clans are fighting once more. He's become increasingly sensitive to warring clans with his regency constantly being challenged by the bairn Queen Mary's mother. Marie de Guise is threatening to bring all of France down on Arran's head."

The politics alone surrounding Scotland were enough to drive a man to drink. "And how has Arran taken your title as Guardian of Scotland?"

Logan let out a long, tired-sounding sigh. "He is still lukewarm about it, but understands that it's best for me to remain the guardian. I know the Highlands and the clans better than he ever will. But he's increasingly tight regarding reining them all in. News of the MacDonalds continual plans of usurping myself and then the crown will not go over well."

"Then we'd best dispatch of this before he gets wind of it."

"My thoughts exactly," Logan said with a frown.

"If we capture the Butcher and send his head back to the MacDonald chief, will that suffice?"

Logan slowly nodded. "Aye, for now."

"I'll assemble the men. The Butcher cannot have gotten too far in less than a sennight." The man had eluded them thus far, but no more. Ewan wouldn't sleep until he was in chains.

"Unless by galleon," Logan said.

"Have the scouts reported use of any suspicious galleons?"

"None other than those reported for trade. But that doesn't mean that the Butcher did not pay, bribe, or threaten his way on one of those."

Ewan nodded. "Then we'll question all the captains."

The dull ache in his chest returned when Ewan realized returning to Shona might take longer than he wanted. The longer it took, the more chance she had of running into one of the MacDonald men herself.

"Assemble the men and give them their assignments, then go to her. Ye'll not work with a clear head until ye know she's safe," Logan said. "But as soon as she's safe behind these walls, we need ye."

"How did ye—"

Logan waved his hand. "I know the signs and symptoms of a captured heart." Then he pointed a finger at Ewan and narrowed his gaze. "And dinna repeat those words to anyone. I like the men to believe I'm heartless."

Ewan grinned. He'd not tell a soul, but that wouldn't help his laird's wishes. The men all knew he had a soft spot when it came to his wife.

"My thanks," Ewan said. "Ye have my word, the Butcher will soon be no more."

Logan groaned. "Quit thanking me and go and get her."

Ewan nodded and hurried from the room. Husband or nay, he was going to bring Shona back to the castle and convince her to leave that life behind.

CHAPTER TWELVE

OUTSIDE the sounds of galloping hooves made Shona's heart leap into her chest. Had Ewan returned? Was that too much to hope for?

She leapt from her bed and made her way toward the door, only noticing at the last minute that the approaching riders were more than one beast. Belly doing a flip, she jerked her hand away from the wooden slat barring the door and backed slowly back to the bed where she'd hidden Ewan's dagger and her bow and arrows.

Wrapping her hand around the hilt, she shoved the dagger through her belt, along with her own, then slung her quiver full of arrows over her shoulder and nocked two arrows in the bow. She stood near the hearth, eyes on the door, arms locked out, the tips of her arrows aimed, and waited.

Her breaths came in ragged, shaky spurts. She tried to slow her breathing, but nothing seemed to help. Since the day Rory had left, she'd wondered when someone would find her, and when she'd met Ewan, she'd been sure it would be any moment.

A heartbeat later there was a scraping sound on her door, as though someone ran their nails down it, followed by two quick successions of knuckle-raps.

Shona swallowed around the lump that had formed in her throat. She didn't answer, didn't move, other than to continue working to steady her breaths and prepare to shoot whoever it was that had come knocking. Being able to hit her mark depended highly on her breathing.

"We know ye're in there." 'Twas a man's voice, gravelly and deep, and the sound of it itched over her nerves, causing the hair on the back of her neck to rise. "We can see the smoke from your chimney."

Saints... 'Twas not Ewan. She'd held out hope that perhaps he'd come back to her and that the extra horses were there for protection.

Shona swallowed, steadying the sudden hitch in her breath.

Be brave. Strength.

The knocking came again, only this time painfully slow, as though the knocker taunted her. "Open up," he said in a singsong voice. "Open up and let us in…"

Mary mother of God…

Fingers trembling, Shona's aim on the door faltered, and she worked to steady herself, but fear flooded her veins. Her knees knocked together, but she shifted, straightening her legs, refusing to let the madman on the other side of the door in. How many others did he have with him?

Shona shook her head, thrusting out visions of a dozen coarse and horrible outlaws crushing down her door, tossing her things, their hands scratching and pulling at her.

The door rattled, and then banged—as though someone had put their shoulder to the wood. The bar jumped in its iron fasteners but held steady. Even still, Shona jumped back, her nerves firing up and down her limbs. She had to get control of herself or else she'd not be able to focus and shoot whoever it was when he finally did gain entry. And there was no doubt they would gain entry. They would attack her. But she wouldn't be the only one hurt in the fray.

The shutters banged open, and a leering face appeared in each window. Skin that looked to have never seen a bath, teeth that were rotted and black. She could smell their foul odor wafting in.

"She's all alone in here, Butcher!" one of the men—with half his ear missing—turned to shout at, she presumed, the man knocking at her door.

"Come out and play, little mouse," sneered the other one. He reminded her of a drooling wolf poised to attack its prey.

Without hesitating, she lifted her bow, aimed and fired the two arrows. One of the vile creatures leapt back, but the other didn't have the speed and her arrow pierced his eye. He let out a shrill scream, hand flying to the offending shaft, and then he fell out of sight, though his screams did not cease.

That didn't make the man on the other side of the door happy. He shouted orders, and while two more men appeared at her window, she nocked and fired two more arrows, but the men were quick to leap out of the way and her arrows flew out the window without hitting their marks. More than one shoulder banged against her door—or perhaps they'd grabbed a fallen tree as a battering ram. Whatever the case, they were intent on gaining entry.

Shona barely breathed. Her heart leapt into her throat.

She had about a dozen arrows left in the quiver, and more in her trunk, but she wasn't sure she'd have time to reach the chest and refill before the bastards came flying through her window and her door.

"Lord, protect me," she murmured.

Hot tears threatened. Though she'd feared it, no one had come up on her in the wood until Ewan. Her gut twisted and though she didn't want to believe it, she knew instinctively these men were here because of him. Was he hurt? Or had he simply gone back to his life and left her to suffer should his enemies come knocking?

She bit down on the inside of her cheek, refusing to give permission to herself to cry. Tears would not help her. Worrying about Ewan and his intentions, or lack there of, would not help her. Fighting would.

Outside the cabin grew quiet for a moment, and then the man spoke through the door again. "Put away your paltry weapons, lass, and let us in. We will nay bite."

They'd seen her through the window and knew she was alone. They'd not be knocking at her door, banging open her shutters and taunting her if they intended to stop by for a friendly visit. Nay, they were here to hurt her. To take things from her. To leave her for dead. Rory had warned her of that aplenty. And even Ewan had, too, before he'd walked out of her life. Shona ground her teeth, but still didn't reply. They did not deserve an answer from her. They deserved nothing.

"Your silence will not help you." The singsong in his voice had disappeared, replaced with a fury that chilled her bones.

She drew in a heavy breath and nocked two more arrows.

The door shuddered once more as they banged against it. The bar cracked, but didn't fully break. All it would take was one more great shove and her barrier would be breached. Could she bar it with something else? Shona frantically glanced about her room. She could shove the chest in front of the door, but it was only a matter of time before they were able to push past it. Besides, where would she go? There was nowhere to hide. No secret exit. And leaving her post would allow men to attack through her windows with their own arrows, even if they couldn't climb through them.

Again the man's hate-laced voice sounded. "Well, dearie, ye've left us no choice."

What could that possibly mean?

Shona flicked her gaze from the door to the windows and back, waiting for whatever punishment it was the man was going to mete out on her.

At first, there was nothing but silence. And then she smelled it. That acrid scent that all women, men and children feared. *Smoke.* Glancing up, her heart stopped. Smoke curled down from her thatched roof and wound its way around her neck, choking the breath from her lungs. She lost her grip on her bow and dropped down to her knees, trying to get to the air that seemed less filled with smoke. But it didn't matter. They must have set several fires to her roof, causing it to burst entirely into flames.

Shona coughed, her eyes watered, throat burned. She'd either burn to death in the fire, or she'd have to open the door—and die at the hands of the man outside. There were no other choices. The violent undertone to the man's voice was a clear message whatever he had in store for her would not be pleasant.

Death was here for her.

Well, she would not choose the man on the other side of the door. She'd rather die inside her home, a place where she'd found peace if not happiness, than by whatever torture he had in store for her.

Shona lay down on the wooden planks of her floor watching as the smoke grew thicker and the ceiling glowed orange with flames. Perhaps this was the right way to go. She'd lived alone, she would die alone.

As she lay there, tears running down her face and the temperature rising, the door crashed open.

"Nay!" she shouted.

She wasn't dead yet. They couldn't come for her, not now!

Shona curled into a protective ball, trying to sink into the floor and coughing all the while. Rough hands wrenched the bow from her hands and the quiver from her shoulder, practically yanking her arm from the socket. She flailed, kicking, screaming, throwing punches. She reached for her dagger, intent on slicing the hands that gripped her, but the blade was torn from her grip.

They dragged her from the little cottage, her gown catching on something and tearing near the hem. They tossed her into the middle of her yard, and she watched the black acrid smoke rise from her house.

"Stupid bitch."

She could barely see the men through her tear and smoke-blurred eyes. She swiped at her eyes in an effort to clear her vision.

When she did, she saw the end of his boot swinging toward he. He kicked her in the stomach, the pain of it taking what little breath she had. She fell backward, clutching her middle, and then, the man slammed something against her skull.

EWAN leapt onto Bhaltair's barely dry back, forgoing his saddle in his haste to get to Shona.

He'd given the orders to his men to question any and all ship captains near the port and in the village taverns. They were also to take a galleon out into the loch and intercept any outgoing vessels, performing searches on all.

As he rode through the gates, Baodan, Gregor and a dozen other warriors followed. But Gregor deviated toward the village with half the men while Baodan stayed with him.

Ewan nodded a silent thank you to the men for staying with him on his journey into the woods. They'd not made it two miles down the wooded road before they saw thick black smoke curling up into the trees.

"Fire." His heart clenched and a cold chill slithered over his limbs.

The flames looked dangerously close to where he'd left Shona.

He urged Bhaltair into a faster gallop as they barreled down the road and then veered off into the forest. At this speed he was in danger of his horse tripping over a tree root. But the closer they got, the more he knew in his gut that the blaze was coming from Shona's cottage.

"Captain, be careful," Baodan warned. "Could be a trap."

Ewan never fought with emotion. He never galloped headlong into battle without a strategy, and the fact that he was doing so now was alarming. He slowed his horse, and turned to face the men.

"That fire is coming from Shona's cottage. If 'tis a trap, then we'd best be prepared to fight. But if 'tis not and she's stuck inside that burning building, I'm going in after her." With that said he turned Bhaltair about and they were off once more.

He entered the small clearing before her house. "Shona!"

There was no answer from her, and what he saw before him took his breath away.

Her house was a bright orange ball of fire and rubble. There was nothing left of it. Could have been a bonfire if he'd not known it to be a quaint cottage.

"Bloody fucking..." He couldn't even speak. He ran his hands through his hair, tugging, felt the painful sting of tears in his eyes.

Leaping from Bhaltair he approached the fire, unsure of how he could find her in the rubble, but knowing he had to try.

"Captain, dinna," Baodan said. "She's not in there."

Ewan kept walking forward until steady hands gripped his shoulders.

"Ewan, she's not in there," Baodan said again.

He turned on the man and shoved him hard in the chest. "How do ye bloody know that?"

Baodan pointed behind him, and Ewan followed his line of vision. Outside the barn, her pig and goat had their throats slashed, their blood seeping into the dirt.

"Someone was here," Baodan said. "My guess is they took her."

"Took her," Ewan repeated. There was a painful tightening in chest.

"Aye." Baodan turned back to the six warriors with them and issued orders while Ewan approached the barn. He searched inside in case Shona had somehow gotten away and hidden herself. But there was nothing.

Back in the clearing his gaze searched the trees for any sign of her or a clue as to where she'd gone. The men did the same, and then one of them let out a whistle. Ewan bolted toward him.

"Lot of tracks here, sir."

Ewan studied the ground. Indeed, there were dozens of hoof prints in the ground, and though he'd not been with her long, he was certain he would have remembered these from when he'd searched for her before he left.

"The blaze was not lit that long ago, else it would have been ash when we arrived," Ewan said. "They can't have gotten that far. There is only one man who could have done this. His name is written all over it."

"The Butcher," Baodan said.

"Aye, the bloody fucking Butcher. He's a dead man. If he's so much as plucked a single hair from her head, I'm going to cut off his cock and shove it down his throat before I gut him," Ewan said through bared teeth.

"Ye might consider it anyway, Captain. Should we send for reinforcements?" Baodan asked. "We may need them."

Ewan shook his head. "We've not got time. He won't keep her long. He'll allow her to linger until she pleases him no more." God, but he hoped she could muster the courage to keep the man entertained at least until Ewan found her.

Her life depended on it.

CHAPTER THIRTEEN

PAIN seared Shona's head. She tried to reach up to touch the spot, but found her hands wouldn't budge. A tight bond held her stiffly in place at an odd and uncomfortable angle.

She blinked open her eyes, and saw nothing but darkness. Her mouth was dry and her lungs tight. She could barely draw in a breath, and when she did, a racking cough shook her body, made all the more uncomfortable with the realization she was so tautly bound, her coughing yanked against the restraints. Her hands were tied behind her back, knotted closely to her ankles. She was trussed up in a painful position causing her back to bow.

Tears clouded her already impaired vision. Judging from the scratchy feeling on her forehead and cheeks, they'd put a woolen bag over her head. Was that to keep her from seeing where she was going? To instill fear? Her head hurt so bad she was worried about the damage they'd already caused. Was the bag so they didn't have to look at her?

She lay still, wherever she was. Shona reached as far as she could with her hands, feeling the coolness of earth and leaves beneath her fingertips. She was on the ground, probably in the woods. The temperature had cooled slightly, which meant the sun had most likely set. And she had no idea how long she'd been knocked out. Shona listened for the sounds of her captors and caught bits and pieces of conversation somewhere off in the distance.

Was this their camp?

Had to be. They didn't strike her as the type of men who would stop along their journey for a respite. She sniffed, but whatever sense of smell she'd had was still filled with the sharp tang of smoke from her cottage.

She would have mourned the loss of her home, of all her medicinal herbs and salves and the notes she'd taken for which combinations worked best. But there was no time for that. If she were dead, it wouldn't matter at all. She had to figure out a way to escape. They'd not killed her yet, but they would.

Rubbing her wrists together in an attempt to loosen her bindings only seemed to make them tighter. The roping bit into her skin, but the burning and rawness of her flesh was worth it if she could just loosen them and make a run for it.

"So ye've awakened?"

Shona's heart plummeted and the pain in her head increased exponentially. She stilled at the sound of the man's voice who'd been behind her door. The same one who'd hit her. Likely the same one who'd tied her up. Fear snaked along her spine and coiled tight. There'd not been enough time to loosen the bindings. There was no escape for her from whatever it was he had planned.

He nudged her knee with the tip of his boot, and even that simple movement sent a sting through her limbs. "Want me to untie ye?"

Shona gasped, then regretted her audible reaction. She didn't want him to know what she was thinking or feeling. What game was this he played?

She nodded slowly, bracing herself for a blow that didn't come.

The sharp coldness of a blade slid over her forearm, but did not pierce her skin. He left her wrists bound. Instead, the cords at her ankles were sliced and her limbs slowly unraveled. She stretched the painful kinks from her legs and her spine.

Fear collided with the need to survive racing through her, and little hope of getting out of this alive. Coldness settled in her bones.

The man grabbed onto her shoulder and pulled her roughly to her feet. The bag was ripped from her head but no light filtered to her eyes. 'Twas nighttime, and the campfire far enough away that only shadows filled the space between her and the flames. She trembled, her teeth chattering, though it was not that chilly.

The man's gaze raked over her in a way that made her feel dirty. "Need to relieve yourself?" he asked.

Shona nodded, surprised he would even care and wondering what his ulterior motive could be.

He grabbed onto her elbow, his fingers biting into her skin, and dragged her behind a bush. The branches scratched at her arms as she passed. The men in his crew jeered at their disappearing bodies. Saints, but this had to be a trick! He didn't truly plan to let her relieve herself. He only wanted to get her away from the prying eyes of his men so he could rape her. Well, she'd not let that happen! She'd force him to kill her before she ever let him touch her.

Shona cleared her throat and attempted to sound meek. She turned partially around and wiggled her hands. "Will ye untie me?"

The bastard's eyes narrowed as he assessed her. "Nay."

Shona turned back around, trying for pleading. "But—"

"I said, nay."

Saints! He wasn't going to untie her. "Will ye at least give me some privacy? Please?" Though it was dark, and he'd likely not see much, she still didn't want him watching her in such a private act. She didn't want *anyone* to see her that way.

"Nay." His answer was short and followed by a bark of laughter. "Now get on with it else I call over the rest of the men to watch."

She struggled with choosing to hold her bladder, but she wasn't sure how long it would be until he let her go again. Holding it wasn't an option unless she didn't care about messing herself, and she *did* care, a great deal.

Shona would have to make do with tugging up her skirts without his help, and attempt to keep her nude lower half obscured from his vision. Fingers numb, Shona grappled with her skirts finally wrenching the back up enough that she didn't think she'd wet her dress but not far enough up that he would see her bare buttocks. But then squatting down became difficult and she teetered unstably on her still semi-numb ankles.

The man gave a disgusted grunt then grabbed her dress and flipped it over her head, covering eyes.

Shona cried out. "Stop!"

Wrenching her head this way and that, she managed to get the gown off of her eyes, but couldn't stop him from touching her. His cold fingers dug into the bareness of her hips and forced her halfway to the ground. She quaked in disgust and tried to wriggle free.

"Unhand me!"

"Shut your mouth and be grateful. Now get on with pissing."

"I can do it on my own," she ground out, mortified and terrified that the man was touching her, watching her. Lord, how she wanted to curl up in a ball and sob.

Strength. Be strong. The one chant that had gotten her through since she'd arrived on Gealach lands afflicted with no memory.

"I dinna care if ye can do it on your own or nay, I like the view." He squeezed her hips tighter; painful enough that she was certain to have bruises upon the morrow. "Ye're skin is... soft." He pressed his nose to the top of her head and breathed in deeply. "And ye smell... like a lush cunt."

Bile rose in her throat, and she coughed, trying to choke it down before she vomited. The nasty thug was trying to humiliate her. To make her uncomfortable and scared. And it was working. Shona turned her head slightly and stared at him out of the side of her eyes. Should she try to run? Even with her hands tied, she could still bolt. When she was finished, she gritted her teeth and squeezed her eyes shut, fully prepared for him to bend her forward and force himself on her. Her teeth chattered again at the thought.

"Pp... please," she murmured, ashamed at showing her fear in front of this man. Ashamed to beg.

He laughed cruelly and then shoved her forward. She stumbled and just when she'd caught her balance, his boot landed squarely on her buttocks in a painful kick. Shona fell to her knees and, unable to catch herself, landed facedown in the leaves, a fallen branch scratching her cheek.

Instinct took over her thoughts. She wriggled forward, trying to put some distance between the man and herself. But with her hands tied behind her back and her gown catching on forest debris, it was difficult to maneuver her body.

"Ye canna get too far now, can ye, dearie?"

Shona let out a sob as the man fell on top of her, grinding his disgusting member against her bare buttocks and looking for entry. He grabbed her hair, tugging her head back painfully. She clenched all of her muscles tight, bucking beneath him.

"Cease moving or it'll only hurt more," he ground out in her ear. "Do ye know what they call me?"

Shona bit down hard on her lip, refusing to answer. Refusing to even believe this man existed. She pictured herself back in her cottage, grinding her herbs. And in that vision, she saw Ewan lying in bed, only he wasn't ill. This time he was beckoning toward her.

"They call me the Butcher. And I'm going to flay ye alive."

MADNESS consumed him. Ewan and his men were tearing the forest apart as the sun slowly succumbed to night and now they were trying in the dark with makeshift torches.

They'd been able to track the MacDonalds using their prints as far as a riverbed where they must have crossed.

"Bloody fucking hell," Ewan growled, reining in his horse.

Bhaltair flicked his ears back, feeling the anger and frustration coursing through Ewan's body.

"Bastards!" How the hell did they keep getting away from him?

Always one step ahead. Well, not this time. This time, he was going to come crashing down on them. If he ever fucking found them.

He swiped his sword at a branch and the limb crashed to the ground beside his horse causing Bhaltair to flick his tail back and forth—hitting Ewan in the back.

Somehow, the rash violence of slicing the tree calmed his rage enough that he could think. When he gazed out over the riverbed he saw a flicker of light. Another torch? No it was bigger than that—had to be a campfire.

"Douse your torches," he ordered. "Someone has made a camp across the river."

"It has to be the Butcher and his men," Baodan said.

The torches sizzled out as the men dipped them into the water.

"And they have Shona." Ewan urged Bhaltair into the water intent on crashing in on their camp. A niggling in his gut bade him to quickly stop. He had to start thinking with his head and not his heart. Crashing through the river wouldn't save her. It would only alert the bastards he was coming and they'd ride off. "We canna get to them this way," he muttered. "They will see us coming."

"Aye, Captain," Baodan said. "I believe the bed thins out a mile north."

"I remember that as well. Let us go and cross there. We'll sneak up on their camp from the north. Take them all out while they sip their whisky and jerk their cocks."

Ewan stared out over the water a moment longer. Their fire still blazed, so they'd not caught sight of the torches, nor heard them speaking. Dear god, he hoped that Shona was all right. For every wound the Butcher and his men inflicted upon her, he would see it reciprocated to them tenfold.

CHAPTER FOURTEEN

THEY crossed the water two miles up instead of one as they'd planned, since the rainstorms earlier in the week had left the river fuller than usual. The wind shifted, sending a welcome blast of air over Ewan's sweat-covered body.

Their horses picked their way carefully through the shallow water, barely make a splash as they went. Careful to stay hidden from any MacDonald scouts, they crept slowly toward the camp. The closer they got, the more he could hear the sounds of men moving about, their low chatter and the occasional snort of a horse.

A female voice caught his attention—her sharp shout, "*Nay*," chilled his blood.

He shot his gaze toward Baodan, waiting for his man to restrain him from surging forward. The wait was not long. They surrounded him, and a hand was placed on Bhaltair's reins.

"Let us count our enemies first," Baodan murmured.

Ewan gritted his teeth, staring into the dimness of the woods, noticing for the first that the moon was full allowing him to see more than he normally would without a torch. At least the sky was cooperating with them.

Meanwhile, the sounds of more than one female in distress drifted from the camp making not just himself, but all the men, tense with the need to pound the bloody MacDonalds into the ground.

Three of his men fanned out to count the blackguards at the camp, and when they returned, their hands glistened with blood.

In low tones, they gave their report. "We took out the lurking scouts. There are over a dozen men around the campfire, some sleeping by the trees, and others... engaged. But no sign of the Butcher."

"What of a fiery-haired lass?" Ewan asked.

"There are several lasses..." The guard trailed off, shifting his gaze from Ewan's.

"Fuck," Ewan said, he knew what that meant.

The jackanapes were engaged... Bloody hell, the bastards were violating the women as they spoke, and

Shona could very well be one of them. Thank goodness for the assistance of the other warriors. They were about to head straight into battle and though he could take on more than one man at a time, he wouldn't be able to defeat a horde of MacDonalds no matter how angry he was.

"We go now," Ewan said.

Ewan signaled the men to surround the camp, and he himself circled around to the southern side of the camp. They split up. Without a second thought, Ewan yanked his claymore from the scabbard at his back. No battle cries were called. They rode soundlessly into the camp, dispatching of MacDonald maggots along the way.

By the time they'd made it through the first ring of wretches, the ones closer to the fire had gathered up their weapons and were prepared to fight.

Ewan whirled his sword in the air, a grin of bloodlust on his lips as he prepared to take out at least five more of the wastrels, but a sound in the bushes beyond the camp drew Ewan's attention. The noise couldn't be pinpointed, but the enemies surrounding him picked up on his attention and moved to stand between him and the din beyond the bushes. He arced his sword in the air, taking out one and then a second of the MacDonald bastards intent on sending him to his grave. The third ducked, but found his end beneath Bhaltair's raised hoof.

"Good, boy," Ewan crooned.

He whipped Bhaltair toward the bushes. What he broke in on took his breath and replaced it with angry fire. Ewan bellowed his outrage. His chest filled with the burning rage.

The Butcher stood with Shona, her hands tied behind her back and her skirts bunched around her waist and slung over his arm. He had a blade at her neck and another hovering over the curls of her sex.

The bloody bastard laughed low and evil. "Is this what ye're looking for? Take another step and I'll slice her pretty cunt into ribbons and then I'll slash her from ear to ear. Ye can watch her bleed while I fuck her into hell."

Ewan gritted his teeth, dismissed the plummet of his belly, his gaze catching Shona's. Even though tears filled her eyes, there was still spirit there. The bastard hadn't broken her yet. But Ewan might with the false words he now had to utter. He sent up a prayer that she'd forgive him for what he was about to say.

Screwing up his face into feigned disgust, he laughed. "What makes ye think I came for the girl?" Ewan pointed his sword at the Butcher. "There are plenty of cunts at the local tavern for fucking. Why would I waste my time on this sorry wench? I came for ye, Butcher. Toss that hussy aside and fight me like a man."

The Butcher's gaze faltered, and then he shoved Shona to the ground. Ewan forced himself not to leap down and catch her before she landed face first in the dirt. It was one of the hardest things he'd ever done.

"Get off that horse ye limp cock and I'll show ye how a real man fights." The Butcher grinned, showing a missing canine tooth he'd most likely lost biting into one of his victims.

Shona scrambled behind a tree, far enough away that the Butcher couldn't get to her before Ewan, but not far enough away in his own opinion. He wanted her sheltered at Castle Gealach. The sooner he gutted this bastard, the sooner he could get her to safety.

"*Fuirich*," Ewan said, making sure Bhaltair remained where he was and ready to assist when and if he gave a signal.

Keeping his eye on the Butcher, he dismounted and stepped forward. A scar raked jaggedly across his enemy's face and Ewan swore by the time this fight was over, he was going to make a matching mark on the opposite side.

"I'm going to watch ye bleed," Ewan said.

"That I doubt." The Butcher gave a smug grin, which Ewan returned.

The bastard was too full of himself. Arrogance was never rewarding and Ewan was going to use that to his full advantage. Battle, wars, and summits were all best fought with the mind first, and then brute force.

They circled each other; neither taking a jab, while off behind them sounds of swords clashing, bones crushing and men dying rang out. Was the Butcher taking Ewan's lead or was he smarter than he'd given him credit for?

"Make your move," the Butcher said, his smirk growing wider. "I can circle ye for hours."

Ewan sneered. "As can I."

"Then we'll be weary—"

But Ewan cut him off, striking forward with a dagger he whipped out of his belt. Butcher jumped back, but not in time. The tip of the blade caught him on his chest, tearing through the fabric and slicing him shallowly above his nipple.

The Butcher feigned indifference. "Where did ye learn to fight? At the brothel with your whore of a mother?" The Butcher grabbed his prick and waggled it.

Ewan blew out a sad breath. Even in a life and death situation the arse made time for cocky jabs. And that one, never felt good. Ewan couldn't remember his mother. In fact, he couldn't remember much before he met Logan as a lad. It was very well possible that she was a whore, which meant anytime anyone said anything negatively about her, he grew angry.

"The only whores I learned anything from were your mother and your sisters," Ewan taunted.

"Enough babble, I'm going to kill ye now." The man quit circling and advanced.

Ewan was ready for him. He'd built up enough strength in his wrists and forearm to use his long claymore one handed and his dagger in the other. Without the skill, he would have had to fight two-handed with his claymore because of the length. That wouldn't do fighting the Butcher. This jackanapes was likely to pull a viper from his sporran and thrust it in Ewan's face, or worse, divide into four like a demon and attack him from all sides. That was the only explanation for a man as vile as the Butcher—that he was spawned from the devil.

Their swords clashed, sparks flying with the force of the connection. Ewan centered his concentration on the man before him. The Butcher was a skilled fighter, better than most. That fact had been obvious with how long he'd survived and been employed by the chief of the MacDonald clan. There were no tales told from the lips of men who'd fought against him, only from those who'd witnessed the Butcher's devastation.

Ewan was not going to lose. His tale of victory would come from his own lips and he'd send the man's head to his master in a chest.

The sounds around them disappeared as Ewan focused in on his goal—kill the Butcher. He advanced, parried, struck and retreated. Vengeance filled him. He fought for every innocent victim who'd succumbed to the devil's sword, fists or other weapons. He fought for Shona, and for what he'd seen and what he didn't see. Ewan's blade sliced into the Butcher's shoulder, his arms, his hands. He ducked from the man's increasingly angry attacks, using his dagger to slice at his enemy's legs.

He managed to avoid most of the devil's counter-attacks, taking a few minor scratches and the brunt of a sword-hilt against his jaw.

The Butcher had been undefeated until now. Probably because the anger he had at the world overshadowed his foes' own wills to live. Or because he was vicious enough and trained enough to see his will be done.

But not with Ewan. It had only been a matter of time before Ewan found him and showed him that there was another with more power and skill to take him down.

'Twas a simple fact — Ewan was the better warrior. To that end, he couldn't help but taunt his foe.

"What is your true name, Butcher? What name shall we call ye when we send prayers to God that he doesn't receive ye at his pearly gates?"

"Ye needn't bother as I am Death and I have come for ye."

Ewan gave a slight shake of his head. The man would be in denial until the end.

With a twist and duck, and quick jab to the right, Ewan leapt into the air and used the full force of his power to kick the Butcher square in the chest.

The foul-mouthed bastard stumbled back, eyes wide with shock. He'd not expected to be overpowered by Ewan. Doubt began to cloud his eyes. This only made Ewan's smile widen.

The arsehole would be dead within the next few minutes.

Seeing his end nearing, the Butcher opened his mouth spewing insults and threats. "The MacDonald will only send another in my place. Ye get rid of me, expect several more, bigger, stronger and badder than I am."

Ewan laughed at the man. "Ye greatly underestimate the Grants. We'll never surrender. And we fight a hell of a lot better than ye cock-sucking MacDonalds. 'Tis why your chief has to continue to send imbeciles like yourself—because ye never triumph."

Butcher roared his rage coming violently toward Ewan with slashing strokes meant to kill. Though each swipe of his sword sent a waft of air across Ewan's face and limbs, the man's weapon never connected. Used to the way the Butcher swung and struck, Ewan was quick, sidestepping, ducking and blocking. When the Butcher appeared to tire, that's when Ewan went on the offensive. He lunged forward, ready to strike the man down. He'd figured out his weak spots and took advantage of it. He arced his sword down on the left, putting as much power into it as he could muster. When Butcher blocked the blow, his teeth gritting and sweat pouring from his face, Ewan stabbed his dagger with his right hand into the man's ribs, piercing his heart.

Butcher's mouth fell open, his eyes widened in disbelief and a small sound of surprise blew past his whitened lips.

"I win," Ewan said through bared teeth.

He yanked his dagger from the man's body, wiping the excess blood on the front of the bastard's shirt, and then pushed him to the ground.

The Butcher gurgled as he fell backward, his gaze at the sky. He clutched at the spreading stain on his shirt, and then stared angrily at Ewan. Despite his injuries, the Butcher still managed to hold his sword out.

Normally, a dying man trying to protect himself until his final breath — enemy or no — would have received Ewan's mercy. But not this day. Ewan knocked the Butcher's sword from his weakened hand and pressed his own blade to the vile man's throat.

"Ye should have stayed north."

With both hands on the hilt, he raised his sword and brought it down hard on the man's neck, severing his head. Blood spurted, mixing with the earth. He only wished he could see the bastard's soul as it sank down to the very depths of hell.

Gripping the head by the hair, he pulled it from the ground, intent on putting it in a bag and sending it back to the northern isles where the MacDonald clan hailed. But when he did, he happened to look up and see that Shona was no longer behind the tree where she'd crawled.

"Shona?" he said, panic rising.

Had someone come up behind her and taken her while he was so intent on fighting the Butcher?

Ewan ran the several yards toward the camp, finding every one of his men either wiping their swords, dragging the enemy bodies to a pile or partaking in the deceased party's bounty. The women who were being raped when they'd arrived were huddled together with Grant plaids around their shoulders and Baodan was handing them a waterskin, hopefully filled with whisky.

A quick glance did not turn up Shona. "Has anyone seen the fiery-haired lass? Shona?"

He hated the panic in his voice, but he couldn't help it. He was deathly afraid of what could have happened to her.

Baodan strode toward him. "Was she here?" Then he glanced down at the head still clutched in Ewan's bloody hand. "Is that him?"

"Aye." Ewan thrust the head toward Baodan. "Wrap it up. We'll bring it to Laird Grant. He'll want to see for himself."

Baodan took the head. "Aye, Captain."

Ewan whirled from the group of men and doubled back to where he'd fought the Butcher. He searched for signs of Shona by the tree, but in the dark it was hard to see much of anything. He dropped to his knees, looking at her prints carefully and then trying to see if he could follow them.

A sound at his back had him leaping to his feet, but all he could see where the shadows of trees and the glowing eyes of an owl not far above him.

"Shona!" His voice broke with emotion. Where *was* she? "Shona!"

CHAPTER FIFTEEN

"EWAN, I am here…"

Shona stumbled out from behind a tree she'd run to while Ewan had been fighting the horrible devil. Though she'd not been in imminent danger in the place she'd first sought refuge, the sounds of the fighting in the camp behind her combined with the sight of Ewan fighting for his life proved too much. She'd had to run. Had to go to a place where she felt safer. A place where she'd not be attacked by any of the Butcher's vile crew should they escape any of Ewan's men, and a place where she couldn't see the Butcher hurt Ewan.

Every slice on his skin, she'd felt bone deep.

"Oh, god, Shona!" Ewan ran toward her, arms outstretched. "I'm so glad ye're safe. I'm sorry for those wretched things I said, I meant none of it."

Still shaking, she grabbed hold of him for balance. "I know. I know."

The moon penetrated the trees and shone down on Ewan in silver strips of light, illuminating his figure. Shivering, she tried to ignore the blood on his clothes and skin, but it was deeply ingrained within her to search for signs of injury.

"Are ye hurt?" She raked her gaze over him, not able to decipher if he was wounded in the dark.

There was so much blood…

"Naught but a scratch, love." He unpinned his plaid, wrenched off his shirt and wiped the blood from his hands onto the fabric before discarding it on the ground. "See?" He turned in a circle for her inspection.

All she could see was that his bandages were clean and he didn't appear to be in any danger of dying. A long breath escaped her and then the shaking worsened. First in her legs and then her arms, her hands. She wobbled, in danger of collapsing.

Ewan tugged her closer into his arms. "Och, love, everything will be well now." Doubt crowded his tone.

Shona laid her head against his chest, letting the warmth of him seep into her cold bones. She wrapped her arms around his waist, feeling safe at last. The past several hours had been hell. And thank god the Grant warriors had arrived in time, else the Butcher would have made good on his threat to penetrate her in more ways than one.

"Are ye all right, lass? How did he hurt ye?" Ewan's doubt was replaced with fear. He cupped the sides of her face and searched her gaze.

"My head hurts, and my wrists and ankles, but the rest of me will heal." She breathed in his scent, letting it wrap its way around her, cocooning her in a safety net that was all Ewan. Her trembling started to subside and the chills racking her slowed.

"*Mo chridhe*, I am so sorry. I should not have left ye." The guilt and regret in his tone struck her in the center of her heart.

Shona pressed her hand to his chest, feeling the subtle thump of his heartbeat beneath her palm. "But ye had to," she said. "I do not hold it against ye."

He pressed kisses to her cheeks and forehead, breathing her in. "I should have insisted that ye come with me."

"To the castle? Nay, I canna," she said, shaking her head against his chest.

"Is this about your husband?"

Shona pulled away from him, gazing into his eyes. "Husband?" She'd told him once before in his fevered state that there was no husband, but he must not have remembered. That made sense. The things he'd said to her before he'd stormed off, his angry reaction. He'd thought she was a woman taken. "I have no husband."

Ewan gripped her upper arms, his brow furrowed. "What?"

Shona smiled weakly at his disbelief. She could have been offended, could have been angry that he would jump to that conclusion, but she wasn't. What woman *would* be out in the woods by herself with no husband?

"I have no husband."

"Were ye widowed?"

That she didn't know. She could have been before coming to Gealach, but it didn't matter now. She'd left that strange, distant and unknown life behind.

Choosing to deny anything in her past, she said, "Nay."

Ewan's eyes squinted as he soaked in her answer. "What of the man's things I saw at your cottage?"

"They belonged to Rory. He was… my friend."

"Your friend?" Ewan looked at her skeptically. "Not your lover?"

"Aye. He rescued me in the wood some years before and he helped me. We were never lovers."

"What happened to him?" Ewan unfortunately sounded like he knew what befell Rory.

"He disappeared…" She shook her head and chewed her lip afraid to ask but forging ahead. "Do ye know something?"

"Och, love, I—"

But they were interrupted by a large warrior looking just as bloody as Ewan, though not seeming to suffer from any injuries either.

"Captain, shall we make a camp or light torches and ride back to Castle Gealach?"

Ewan glanced back at Shona. "Light the torches. I'll not stay another moment where these blackguards made camp."

"But, Ewan, I—" Shona started.

He cut her off with a curt shake of his head. "Ye're coming with me, lass. I hate to be the bearer of such news, but your home is gone. Your animals…"

Shona closed her eyes, willing herself to be strong. "I know. I saw. I…"

"Ye'll come back to the castle with me." His voice held no room for argument.

She opened her eyes and met his gaze. She was going to argue anyway. "But I canna."

"Why, woman?" Frustration crinkled the corners of his eyes. "There is nothing left for ye here. Ye have no place to go. I'm offering ye something greater than what ye have."

She tried not to feel angry at his choice of words. "The people, they… dinna trust me." Where *would* she go? Wherever it was, she'd have to leave Ewan behind, the thought in itself painful.

"I have already spoken to his lairdship. He has approved of ye coming to the castle. He says ye can be the castle healer."

The news was startling. Did this mean…? Could it possibly be that Ewan had come back in search of her, not just the Butcher and his men? Her heart skipped a beat at the thought and hope bloomed in her chest.

"Do ye…" She trailed off and took a deep breath, summoning the courage to ask. "Do ye want me to come to the castle? To live there?"

"Lass, I want so much—"

Behind them the man returned and cleared his throat. "Begging your pardon, Captain, the men have loaded the lasses we found onto the MacDonald horses as well as all bounty. Torches have been lit. We are ready to depart when ye give the order."

"We come anon." Ewan glanced at Shona, studying her. "Are ye ready, lass? Ye can start anew."

Starting anew only five years after she'd done so did not appeal to her.

"Nay, I will not start over again," she said. "This is but another path in the road of my life. I will continue on."

Ewan held out his hand. "I hope we can continue on *together*."

A warm glow flowed through Shona. "Aye, 'haps we can." Was he offering to her what Rory had, or was it something deeper?

She couldn't tell, and with his guard standing close she didn't want to question him only to find out that wasn't what he had in mind. So, she took his hand, letting his large grip encompass hers and allowing his strength to seep into her.

Ewan led her toward Bhaltair, who nickered when he recognized her. Shona patted him on his forehead, rubbing that spot between his eyes that she knew he liked.

"Ye've ruined my horse," Ewan said. "The beast has never greeted anyone besides me until he met ye."

Shona smiled. "He's a sweet horse."

Ewan grunted. "He's yours now. Canna have a sweet horse to take into battle."

Shona clucked her tongue. "Dinna let him hear ye say such."

He reached for her, gripping her around the waist and lifting her as though she weighed nothing. He leapt onto the horse behind her, shifting her to sit on his lap, her legs dangling over his.

His thigh felt hard beneath her buttocks, and the warmth of his body seeping into hers reminded her of all the precious moments they'd shared inside her cottage. She yearned for more of those moments with him. Shona snuggled against him, wanting to savor the ride back to the castle, because she didn't know if she'd get him to herself again.

Aye, he'd said he wanted to walk the road with her, but she didn't know what that meant. If she were going to be a healer in the castle, and already on edge with the townsfolk thinking her a witch, then she had to protect her reputation. She couldn't be seen gallivanting around with Ewan, no matter how much her heart and body yearned for him. A woman's reputation was the most valuable thing she had, Rory had taught her that.

And she needn't give the clan and townsfolk fodder for their wagging tongues.

One of the reasons Rory had kept her at arm's length—he was afraid of ruining her reputation. She'd understood it, even if there had been a time when she wanted to be closer. After meeting Ewan, she'd realized that the feelings she'd harbored for Rory weren't a thing of the heart, nor a deeper attraction that stirred her blood. She'd thought she was supposed to feel something for him. After all, he'd saved her. Mayhap that had to do with her doubt in Ewan's feelings. Did he only offer to bring her to the castle, to be with her, because he felt obligated?

Shona tried to shift forward, determined to get away from all of his heat. Already, her body was responding and making her lose sense, which was wholly inappropriate considering that she'd been held down by a complete monster, and the dead lay in a pile to their left. But Ewan wrapped his arm around her waist and yanked her back flush against him.

Her nipples tightened and between her thighs tingled, growing damp with the anticipation of something that would not come.

Nettles, but the man made a wicked wanton out of her.

Ewan urged his horse forward. Men flanked them on both sides and behind, holding torches to light their way through the woods. They crossed over a shallow body of water, the men whispering prayers that no water beasts or nymphs would come up to capture them as they went.

They made it safely to the other side and then Ewan ordered them all into a gallop.

With nowhere to go, and Ewan not letting her lean away from him, Shona sank against his warm, bare chest. She closed her eyes and imagined that Ewan was hers and hers alone.

All the chills that had seeped inside her the moment the foul demons had knocked on her door dissipated. A strong sense of calm filled her. From here on, things would be different. There would be much she'd need to learn about living in a castle. But she knew her trade well, and she was certain she could gain the respect of the people quickly, if only they wouldn't think her a witch. Maybe that was where Ewan could help her.

"I hope ye'll forgive me," Ewan whispered in her ear.

"There is nothing to forgive." She turned her head enough that she could look up at him without having to sit forward.

Stubble covered his strong jaw, and his lips were curved slightly in a grin, though there was much more to that small turn of lips than happiness. She saw question, hope, fear, relief.

"I feel differently, *mo chridhe.*" He pressed his lips to her head, and inhaled deeply.

'Twas the second time he'd called her *his heart*. He'd also called her *love*. The terms of endearments tugged at her heart, made her belly do a little flip. They made her feel hope she wasn't certain she should have. Ewan didn't strike her as the type of man who threw out meaningless endearments. But could she trust them? She'd been alone for so long, it was hard to know whether her instincts were accurate or not.

"Ye dinna owe me anything, Ewan. I did not save ye because I expected anything in return." She chewed her lip and glanced at the men around them, hoping they couldn't hear what she was saying. "Nor did I consent to make love with you because I had hoped to gain something from it."

Ewan growled low in his throat. "I'd never think such about ye. When I said those things back at your cottage, I didna mean them. I was angry. I was jealous. Ye see, Shona, I want ye for my own. When I came back to find ye, I was determined to steal ye away from the outlaw ye'd married."

Shona was struck by what he'd said. Elation filled her chest, but at the same time, confusion and dread. "Outlaw?"

What exactly did the Grants believe about Rory?

"Aye, lass. Rory MacLeod was a wanted man."

CHAPTER SIXTEEN

"YE'RE mistaken," Shona said, her voice shaking.

Ewan tugged her closer, not wanting her to be upset with him. They rode at an easy lope, their pace quick but not jarring. The sky was inky black and golden stars winked down upon them. The sound of their voices carried over the pound of hooves in an otherwise silent night.

"Nay, lass. His chief sent a missive to Laird Grant."

"Then his chief lied." Conviction dripped from her words. "Rory was a good man. He didna deserve whatever happened to him."

Shona sounded close to tears causing guilt to sour Ewan's belly for having been the one to make her feel that way.

"Ye knew him well?" he asked softly.

"Aye, verra well these past five years. He was not an outlaw. He was kind. He was fierce, but with purpose. He planned to approach Laird Grant with his story and ask for a place within his guard."

That did not sound at all like what he'd heard, but Ewan trusted Shona. If she believed this than it was worth examining. "What happened?"

Shona shrugged and sank further into him, as though she wanted to disappear. "He left to buy a mule. Thought it would help us with preparing our small garden and harvest. But he never returned."

The man would have most likely traveled to Gealach village or a nearby town during one of the market days. Any number of people could have seen him.

"When?" Ewan asked.

Shona crossed her arms over her chest, her elbow resting on his own arm. "Nearly two years past, now."

"And ye've been alone all this time?" Great sorrow seeped into his voice. He couldn't imagine her being left alone. She deserved so much better than that.

"Aye."

She was even stronger than he first realized. "How did ye survive?"

"My trade."

"Healing?"

Pride filled her voice when she answered. "Aye, 'tis why some people thought I was witch. I am exceptionally gifted."

And she was.

"Uneducated peopled dinna understand the difference between knowledge and sorcery. They will soon learn the truth."

She shrugged again, but said nothing. He could practically feel the doubt rolling off of her in waves. She didn't think they would accept her. Didn't think she'd make it in the village or the castle.

Her doubt pained him, because he wanted everything to be perfect for her.

"I'll see that ye are welcomed. And our laird has said he'll see to it as well."

"Ye mentioned that. But how?"

"Trust me, Laird Grant has his clan well in hand. They trust him, Shona, and ye should, too."

"I wish that I could." She turned slightly to study him. "'Tis not that I wish to give your laird any disrespect, only that it has been verra hard for me to trust anyone over the years."

Ewan worked to thrust his frustration aside. Having been in her situation once before, he tried to find the right words to say. "I will make things right for ye. That I promise."

She smiled. "I know ye will try, and I appreciate it. But I also have to find my own way. When I came to Gealach, I hid behind Rory, and then when he was gone, I hid behind the trees and the kindness of those who sought me out. I canna hide forever."

"Ye're brave. Braver than ye know," Ewan said.

A soft laugh escaped her. "If ye say so."

"I dinna only say it to hear the sound, lass. Words should never be uttered without meaning."

She glanced up at him again and he found his heart flooding with warmth at the trust in her eyes.

"Then I thank ye, warrior."

They came to the end of the woods and across the moors the village lay sprinkled beneath a vast star-peppered sky. Lights from torches lit the high thick stone wall that circled the bailey and main stone keep. Castle Gealach. The impressive sight always brought him both chills and a thrill. This place he called home. This place that had changed his life.

"We're almost there," he said.

Nodding to his men, they continued their brisk pace over the soft dewy grasses until they came to the gate.

"Ewan Fraser," he called up to the men, who quickly raised the portcullis and opened the massive double wooden doors, their iron hinges cranking.

"Welcome back, Master Fraser," the gatekeeper called down.

The men rode through the opened gate into the lower bailey, greeted by a couple of guards and several groomsmen who'd been roused to complete the care of their horses.

"A special treat for Bhaltair," Ewan ordered. The poor beast had worked hard to get him to Shona's cottage and then to the camp and back.

He dismounted from the horse and then reached for Shona. His fingers spanned her tiny waist and he lifted her, remembering how much he liked the feel of her in his arms. As he slid her — rather indecently — down his body, her lush curves molding against his hard contours, he gave her a wicked grin.

"Welcome to Castle Gealach."

Shona flashed him a saucy smile in return. "Will every dismount be as… enticing as this one?"

Ewan laughed. "Only if 'tis me."

"Why, of course." With a coquettish tilt of her head she skirted around him. From all outward appearances, she seemed unafraid of where they were and the rumors that surrounded her. That was one of the things he found himself drawn to — her bravery, her ability to forge ahead.

Blast, but he'd fallen hard for the chit.

And why did he get the sense that she was teasing him with that brazen look? A glance meant to rouse his manly bravado. Probably because she was. There was never a dull moment where Shona was concerned.

"Captain." Baodan stood beside him holding out a thick woolsack.

Ewan eyed it, knowing the contents. With a nod he took the sack, noting that his men had done a good job wrapping the head, as no blood dripped from the bottom.

"Baodan, see Lady Shona to my chamber while I go and speak to his lairdship."

Shona jerked her gaze toward him, fear in her eyes. Ewan gently took her hand in his and squeezed. Lord, but he wanted so badly to brush his lips over hers.

"I'll nay be long, and Baodan will see ye safely to my chamber. Bar the door if ye like when ye get there," he said.

Inching close to him, she whispered, "Will I not have my own room? What will they think?"

Ewan glanced down at her, an understanding smile on his lips. "They will think naught of it, lass. There is not another room prepared for ye, and I can always sleep with the men."

She nodded, pulling her hand away and tugging the blanket he'd given her tighter around her shoulders. Because the urge grew to be too much, Ewan leaned down and brushed his lips over hers.

"No worries, *mo chridhe*."

Heart lurching, he had to put some distance between them before he took it upon himself to deliver her to his chamber forgetting his duties. He'd been allowed to bring her here on the condition that Logan could count on him, and he wasn't going to let him down.

Ewan strode swiftly toward the keep, taking the stairs to the main doors two at a time. He found Logan in the great hall pacing, several of his men surrounding him and his wife Emma curled up in high-back chair by the hearth.

When he strode through, all talking ceased and Logan barreled toward him. Emma slipped from the great hall, head bowed. He hoped she would seek out Shona and make her feel welcome.

"What happened? Ye were gone overlong," Logan said.

Ewan held up the bag. "A gift for ye, my laird."

"Ye found him?" Logan stared hard at the bag. "Is your lass all right?"

Ewan blew out a deep breath. "Aye, she will be all right. He burned her house to the ground, brutally butchered her animals. She was a little roughed up, but other than that, he was not able to..." Ewan gritted his teeth unable to even voice the words. Bile rose in his throat at the thought of that bastard putting his grimy hands on Shona, violating her body.

Logan drew in a deep breath, his observant regard sweeping over Ewan. "I understand. I'm glad ye made it back in one piece."

Ewan nodded, relief once more flooding through him that Shona had not been harmed. That they were back at Gealach and she was safe.

"He and the men he came with are dead. Shall I have the head delivered to his master?" Ewan asked.

Logan nodded. "We need not bother with formalities. Have it put in a chest with straw and delivered posthaste."

"He may take vengeance on our messenger."

Logan grinned unpleasantly. "Nay, we have two of his men within our dungeon. They'll deliver the head and any news the MacDonald will need."

"War will be unavoidable." Ewan's blood chilled.

Logan's face turned grim. "Aye."

A soft knock on the door startled Shona away from the slitted window she'd been staring out—mesmerized by the star filled sky. And probably in a bit of shock from her ordeal, and new situation.

Had Ewan returned so soon? She'd not expected to see him for a long time. Baodan had said he would send up a maid to see what she needed. Perhaps that was she.

She went to the door but stopped short of taking down the bar. "Aye?" she said loud enough that whoever was on the other side would hear her.

"'Tis Lady Emma, Mistress of Gealach."

The chief's wife?

Shona swallowed hard. What warranted a visit from the mistress? Was she going to tell Shona there had been a mistake and she needed to leave? A shiver rolled over her skin and dread twisted her heart. She supposed she should have known that would happen. She'd been warned before not to come here. Better that the mistress tell her now and see her escorted out before

Ewan returned. She would be completely mortified if he were to see her so undignified.

Taking a deep breath, Shona opened the door for the clan's mistress. The woman on the other side of the door had hair just as fiery-red as Shona's, pulled into a soft bun at the nape of her neck, lochs curling in disarray around her temple. She wore a simple green gown with the Grant sash over one shoulder. She was beautiful, enchanting, even, and her warm blue eyes didn't show the animosity Shona had expected. In fact, the woman smiled warmly.

"Welcome. My name is Lady Emma." She held out her hand not in a way that Shona had seen before, but that she instinctively knew to grip. How she'd come by that information she had no clue.

She slipped her hand into the warm softness that was Emma's and gently shook it. A handshake. That was what it was called, and how did she know that information?

"I'm Shona," she said.

"May I come in?" Emma asked.

Shona nodded and stepped back to allow the woman room to pass. She shut the door behind her, but didn't bother to bar it. With the way the woman had welcomed her, she was suddenly wondering if there would be no need to fear the people of Gealach after all.

"I have a bath coming for you, and a hot meal." Emma's gaze roved over her.

Shona still clutched the plaid around herself. Emma's accent was different than the rest. *Sassenach*, she'd heard some describe her as, but oddly enough, Emma's tongue was more familiar than her own. That was extremely strange. A fresh chill snaked over her as she recalled every strange vision she'd had since arriving here years before. The woman in her peculiar dreams, that she knew to be *herself*, had the same sounding speech as Emma.

"Are you hurt?" Emma asked.

She shook her head, cleared her throat. "Nay, my lady."

"I'm so sorry for what happened to you. I… have been there before."

"With the Butcher?"

Emma shook her head with a pained expression. "Someone else."

"I'm sorry." Shona's heart went out to the woman she'd just met. If anyone had to go through what she'd gone through with the Butcher, they deserved all the sympathy she could muster.

Emma waved her hand. "Oh, there is no need for you to apologize." Emma smiled. "It's all in the past now."

Shona smiled, watching Emma glide silkily toward a chair and sit in it as though she'd stay for tea.

"Where are you from, Shona? I know you've lived in the woods these past few years helping our own healers. But before then, where did you come from? Are you a MacLeod like your companion Rory?"

Emma knew of Rory? Did all of Gealach? Shona gave an uneasy nod then shook her head, confused herself about her origins and too exhausted to think more clearly.

"If you are, I promise I won't bite."

A knock cut off Shona's reply and she watched Emma leap to her feet and rush to the door. Several servants carried in a bath, linens, soaps and a change of clothes, followed by buckets of steaming water and platters of succulent scented food and wine.

Her stomach growled. She was definitely hungry, but she yearned more for a bath than food at the moment. The need to scrub away the Butcher's filthy touch was intense. Though he'd not been able to rape her, he'd still touched her with his rotten prick and hands.

After the servants left, Emma poured her a glass of ruby-colored wine and handed it to her.

"Take a sip and then get in the tub. I'll wash your hair."

Shona felt odd about letting Emma bathe her, but was suddenly too exhausted to argue. She took a deep sip of the wine, letting the liquid slide down her throat and settle warmly in her belly.

Emma turned her back. "Go ahead and undress. Let me know when you're in the water."

"Thank you," Shona said, noticing the change in her voice, her pronunciation of *ye/you*. She flinched, unsure of what was happening.

Her entire world felt like it was spinning faster and faster out of control. Like a whirlwind that scooped up everything in its path, and left destruction in its wake. She hoped she was sturdy enough to withstand it.

Strength. Be strong.

She shucked her clothing and then stepped into the warm water, unable to stop herself from letting out a little moan of pleasure. It had been so long since she'd taken a real bath — over five years, at least. More than a thousand days since she'd been able to submerge into a warm tub.

"I'm in," she said after settling down and leaning her head back on the rim. "This is heavenly. Thank you so much for your hospitality."

Emma cleared her throat and stepped closer to the tub. "Shona… Your accent, it has changed."

Shona bit down hard on the inside of her cheek. Emma had noticed? The Mistress of Gealach would certainly thrust her out into the night now.

Shona shook her head in answer, unwilling to say another word. Emma crooked her head to the side, studying her with squinted eyes.

"There is something different about you, Shona, then the rest of the Highlanders I've met. I can't seem to put my finger on it."

"'Haps 'tis only that I'm not from here." She worked to keep her Scottish accent in place.

"Yes, I think that is so, indeed." Emma turned around and handed her back her glass of wine. "Take another sip, because I need to ask you a very serious question."

Shona's eyes widened as she stared at Emma. The Mistress of Gealach stood tall, her face void of emotion, but there was knowledge in her eyes that Shona found intimidating.

Drawing in a deep gulp, Shona attempted to push aside her anxieties. But they persisted. Had Emma had only bribed her with sweet warm water and wine in order to inform her of the bad news that she'd have to leave.

"Wh... What is it?" Shona asked.

Emma tilted her head, observing her with a steady stare. "Where are you *really* from?"

Shona shook her head, her lower lip trembling. "I don't know. You've asked me that already."

Emma ignored her. "Your accent—it has changed since you started talking to me. You know how to shake hands. You're different than everyone else. Much different. Tell me, do you have dreams of... anything odd?"

Shona swallowed around the lump that had formed in her throat. How did Emma know of her visions? She chose to deny it. "Yes, I... We *all* have dreams."

Emma came forward with the jug of wine and refilled it, a knowing smile on her lips. She set the jug down and knelt beside the tub. All the determination still squared her shoulders, but there was a softness about her now. And it was *that* gentleness which seemed to put Shona at ease. Could she trust Emma?

"There are dreams and then there are *dreams*," Emma said. "Do you know what year it is?"

"Aye, I've been keeping track. 'Tis 1543."

"How long have you been here?"

"I've been at the castle only an hour, at most." Shona crinkled her brow, uncertain of where this was going, and not necessarily liking it. *Those* dreams that Emma was speaking of were creeping into the forefront of Shona's mind, threatening to take over.

"Shona, I may know where you are from."

Was it possible that this woman had an inkling? Could lead her to the truth of her past? The idea that Emma could help her touched the deep part of Shona that yearned to comprehend. "Where?" she asked, breathless with anticipation.

"Same place as me." Emma's lips flattened and she narrowed her brow, staring deep into Shona's eyes as she said with all seriousness, "This is going to sound mad, but I am from the future— almost five-hundred-years from now. And I think you are, too."

Shona almost laughed. Could have tossed her wine aside and run from the room screaming about the insanity of Emma's words, but she didn't. Instead, Shona grew very still as memory after memory came tunneling back of the strange woman in her visions— *herself*—reading a book and drinking a glass of wine; standing on a boat with thick sails and breathing in the salted air; riding on a large, fast-moving, overlong, iron wagon full of people; frantically scribbling in a journal; and one thing she was familiar with — picking herbs. Except *she* picked herbs in an unnaturally lit domed building, with strange whirring noises, and odd boxy objects. The alternate world. Differences that were both terrifying, and unbelievable. If what Emma said was true...

She stared up at Emma whose gaze had turned unwavering.

"Am I right?" Emma said.

Before she could stop, Shona found herself nodding. "I think that might be what happened to me. But when I got here... I didn't remember anything. Nothing but my name. And now, only bits and pieces that come in flashes I don't understand. Nothing makes sense."

"I'm going to help you. You've adjusted a lot better to time travel than I have, but maybe that's because you didn't know. Well, now that you do" — Emma's smile brightened her features — "I will definitely need to help you. And you'll get through this just fine."

"But... I don't remember." She bit down on the tip of her tongue, staving off tears.

"I'll help you. But for now, just rest. When you're settled, you and I will start working on coaxing your memories out. I want to know everything about you." She paused chewing on her lips and search Shona's face. "This must be so terrifying for you. I remember being so scared. But Ewan is a good man, and he's smitten with you. He'll protect you. Logan and I will protect you. I am glad to have someone like myself here. I..." Emma reached out, tears glistening her eyes, and grabbed onto Shona's wet hand. "You'll get through this. I promise."

Shona held her breath and sank under the water. Everything would be all right? How? It seemed like it had all just gotten infinitely more complex.

Amnesia she could handle. Traveling back in time? Now that was just *too* incredible. She was more likely to believe in witchcraft.

And yet, it appeared to be the answer to so many of her questions.

CLOSE to dawn the following morning, Ewan finally trudged up the stairs to his chamber. Knowing that Emma had seen to Shona's care had helped him to continue his duties for his laird calmly. The Mistress of Gealach, and his dear friend, would have taken excellent care of the woman he intended to marry.

Physically and mentally exhausted, all he wanted to do was climb into his bed and sleep for days.

Opening the door to his chamber, he was struck by the sight of Shona sound asleep in his bed. 'Twas a vision he planned to live with forever and it brought a smile to his face. He'd promised to sleep with the horses, but there was only an hour at most until dawn.

Slipping beside her for that short a time would be all right.

Careful not to wake her, he quietly closed the door, stripped out of his clothes and climbed into bed. She made a soft murmuring noise. Ewan couldn't help himself. He reached for her, sighing with contentment when she cuddled close to him without waking.

The lass trusted him, and that only seemed to make his chest swell with happiness.

"I love ye," he whispered, even though he knew she wouldn't hear him in her sleep. "I love ye so damn much."

CHAPTER SEVENTEEN

THERE were about three minutes before she was fully awake that Shona felt she was in a glorious, heavenly cocoon of safety and love.

And then everything came tunneling back to her. Her conversation with Emma. The newest visions. The realization that she had another life somewhere five hundred years, more or less, in the future. The fact that she didn't really belong here, and if the cosmic phenomenon that brought her here decided she had to go home, there was nothing she could do about it.

Ewan lay behind her, his arm draped over her waist, and legs entwined with hers. He breathed softly in her ear, asleep to the world and to her increasing panic.

Her lower lip took a beating from her teeth as she contemplated slipping quietly from the room to return to the place in the forest where Rory had found her. The only problem was, she had no idea how to return to her time — and she was fairly certain she didn't want to be there.

The previous night, Emma had told her that in the beginning she'd tried to get back to her own era several times and it never worked. What she'd realized in the end was that she belonged here in the 1500's with her husband, Logan.

Shona also felt a strong pull to this place. She'd adapted very easily with Rory's help, and she wanted to stay, wanted to be with Ewan. But if he was not as committed as she hoped... Could she stay? Would it be worth it? An even more pressing question was, would Fate allow her to stay?

Was the year 1543 her destiny? Was Ewan?

"Morning, love," he said against her ear, his voice filled with sleep.

She'd not remembered him coming to bed, but it felt so right in his arms, she didn't want him to leave.

"Good morning."

"What are ye thinking about? Your thoughts are bouncing so hard off your head they are vibrating the walls," he teased.

Shona let out a nervous laugh.

"I was just thinking about ye." She kept the Scottish accent she'd gotten used to using, though she feared when she was around Emma, she might slip into *her* same speech patterns.

Ewan cuddled closer, his arousal, hard and thick pressing against her buttocks. He was *nude*. Gloriously, hotly naked. Shona closed her eyes, allowed herself a moment to enjoy the feel of his strong body. Even now, despite what she knew, her body came alive, craving every part of him.

"What about me?" His voice had lost its sleepy fog and was replaced by a seductive tone.

Shona shivered. "A lady never divulges her secrets," she said.

Ewan chuckled and bit her earlobe sending a thrill of excitement to rush through her veins. Her nipples puckered and between her thighs grew damp and tingly. One word, one touch, and she would strip out of her nightdress and let him do whatever he wanted to her.

"What if I give ye no choice?" he asked.

Curiosity piqued, she raised a brow and smiled. "How would ye do that?"

"Ah, lassie, I have my ways." He tilted his hips forward, pressing his cock harder against her buttocks, and Shona found her mouth watering, skin covered in goose flesh.

Whatever he had in mind, her body was more than ready to accept. Was her mind? Her heart?

That was harder to tell. For certain, every fiber of her being wanted her to give in. Nevertheless, she struggled with what was right and what was a mistake.

Then he slid his tongue over the shell of her ear and whispered, "I want to feel ye writhe beneath me. I want to make ye tremble and hear ye moan. I want to know *all* of your secrets."

Unbidden, a soft whimper left her. Zounds, but the man was already tearing down all of her defenses. Mayhap this one time she could just let herself go? Allow herself to enjoy the moment with this man. That was what she wanted deep down inside anyway, wasn't it?

Aye. She wanted it so acutely, it took her breath away.

"Ewan..."

"Aye, love, dinna deny me. Please, I could nay..." He trailed off, and the depth of emotion that filled his voice when he asked her — nearly begged he — to make love to him, was enough to break down the last of the protective wall she'd tried to build up around her heart.

Where Ewan was concerned, there was no wall. There was nothing she wanted to keep from him and nothing she didn't want to share with him. Unknowingly, he'd become her present and her future.

The past no longer mattered. All that did was that the two of them had this moment, these precious breaths where their heartbeats connected as one and time didn't exist.

Shona rolled over, draping her leg over his thigh and sliding a palm over his corded arm until she reached his cheek.

"I could never deny ye."

Ewan gazed into her eyes and pressed his nose to hers. "If ye did, it would be paramount to torture."

"For us both."

She angled her head enough that she could brush her lips over his, sighing against his mouth.

Every time they kissed it was a delicious escape. Swoon-worthy.

Could her former self say the same? Not a single memory came to her of another man kissing her the way Ewan did.

Wrapping one hand around his back and laying the flat of her opposite palm on his chest, she felt his heartbeat against her fingertips as he kissed her. His tongue slid slowly, tantalizingly over hers.

Intoxicating.

That was what he was to her — a potent aphrodisiac that she couldn't get away from even if she tried. She was thoroughly addicted to Ewan Fraser.

Her heart beat faster, pulse pounding so hard behind her ribs she swore he could hear it. She trembled with the heady craving she'd come to know since first laying eyes on him. Every part of her yearned, strained for him.

"Touch me," she said, believing if he didn't do so soon, she'd perish of unfulfilled anticipation.

"Where?" His palm stroked down her back and over her hip to grasp her buttock.

Her breath hitched. "Everywhere."

"Does that mean ye'll stay?" Ewan pulled back from her lips, his blue eyes exploring hers. "I could not bear to live without ye."

"Aye, I'll stay." She gripped onto him tighter, fearing the swell in her chest, the lump in her throat, as strong emotion took hold. "I dinna want to live without ye, either. But…" Could she tell him the truth about her past? What if she told him and he left her? Thrust her aside? Accused her being the witch he'd denied she was from the beginning?

"I love ye, lass. I love ye so much it hurts inside and I can think of nothing else. I want ye to be my wife."

Shona's whole world flipped upside down in those simple few words he uttered. Her mouth fell open, eyes widened and filled with tears. He loved her? He wanted her to be his wife?

No one had ever felt that way about her. Said those things to her. *Wanted* her. She was fairly certain of it. These emotions swirling inside her were wholly new and wonderful. She would have remembered feeling them before.

Her own need warred with her conscience. And need won out.

She could explain to him later about her time origin. Emma and Logan could help her, but for now she needed to be with him. Needed to make *another* confession.

"I love ye, too, Ewan. I—" She choked on a sob and pressed her lips tightly and briefly to his. "No one has ever made me feel the way ye do. Aye, a thousand times, aye, I will be your wife."

A huge infectious smile split his face, and Shona smiled widely in return.

"We'll be married today."

"Is that possible?"

"If we want it. And ye do, right?"

"Aye, *mo chridhe,*" she said, using his term of endearment. "I do."

Ewan started to move away from her. "I must go make preparations. I must tell Logan."

Shona pulled him back down to her. "Not so fast, warrior. There is something I need first."

His eyes lidded heavily as he raked them over her body, watching her nipples harden on sight. "Och, aye, seems I forgot I have a challenge to complete."

"A challenge?" she giggled.

Ewan grabbed her arms, pinning them over her head. His thighs straddled her own, restraining her.

"Seems a young lassie challenged me to uncover all of her secrets." He dipped low, his teeth grazing over one puckered nipple, eliciting a sharp gasp from her. "What treasure exists here?"

His warm breath seeped through the linen nightdress, the wetness of his mouth on the fabric chilling her and heating her blood all at once. When he

231

moved to her other nipple she arched her back and tried to wriggle free from his grip so she could grab hold and touch him, stroke him.

"*Tsk tsk*, fair lassie. Dinna make me shred this gown and tie ye up."

A shiver skated over her body. Aye, she wanted that very much, but the wounds at her wrist from the Butcher had not quite healed. But maybe, that was what she needed to help wipe away that memory? Needed to replace that heinous event with one filled with safety and love.

"I want ye to," she said, determined.

"I dinna want to hurt ye." He stared at her wrists, his jaw tight in anger at her injuries. "I have another idea."

Ewan climbed nude from the bed and grabbed his belt from the floor. He strapped the belt to the headboard leaving a loop dangling. "I want ye to hold it, but first I need to get ye as naked as myself."

Shona started to grab the hem, but Ewan brushed her hands aside.

"Let me do it, beautiful." His eyes glistened with want, sending a fresh thrill running through her.

Her sex was wet, and the firing bundle of nerves between her thighs throbbed with the need for his attention. She lifted her buttocks in the air as he slowly slid her gown up to her hips, his fingers dragging over her thighs, massaging the skin there, and leaving a wave of goose bumps in his wake.

As he revealed her drenched folds, a wicked grin curved his lips.

"What about down here, lassie? What secrets do ye hold?"

She not only sensed, but also could see, the thrill of his arousal as his cock seemed to grow impossibly harder than it already was.

He bent forward, kissing her hipbone. He trailed his lips, and hot breath, over her belly to her other hipbone where he bit her softly.

Shona groaned, her legs falling open, and a waft of air caressing seductively over her slit.

Ewan skimmed his lips lower, the stubble of his beard scraping erotically over her sensitive skin, but he didn't go right for her pink pearl. He nuzzled her lips, her inner thighs. Teased his tongue around her opening.

Of its own accord, her pelvis angled up. Where her mind had slowly lost its sense, her body knew what it wanted, searching out his tongue to stroke the firing bundle of nerves. Ewan chuckled.

"Eager, lassie, are ye not?"

"Aye," she moaned, gripping tight to the belt loop above her. She wanted so bad to thread her fingers through his hair, to tug tight and force his mouth to her throbbing flesh. He continued to tease her, blowing hot air upon her, then licking, sucking, kissing, brushing his lips over every part of her but that *one* spot. "Please, Ewan."

Back arched, palms cutting into the leather, and legs parted wide, she bucked upward as he finally slicked his tongue over her nub. He flicked. He swirled. He rubbed. When she got used to one pattern, felt her body spark toward a climax, he changed, keeping her forever in a tormented peak without letting her teeter off.

She moaned as she rocked against his face. She slid her feet over his ribs. He gripped each hand beneath her buttocks and lifted her off the bed as he devoured her body like it was his last meal. Shona held tight to the belt like it was a lifeline, but she was dangerously close to letting go of that hold and gripping onto him as though her life depended on it.

"Keep your hands on that belt, but let your body go, love, let me feel your cunny flutter on my tongue." He stabbed his tongue deep into her slit while he scraped his teeth and upper lip gently over her bud.

There was nothing she could do but succumb to the incredible pressure that had built so deliriously inside her. In that one tiny move, her entire body broke apart, trembling madly. Thighs quaked against his face. A gasp that seemed to suck all the air from the room. A pleasure-filled cry that shook the rafters. All the decadent energy that swarmed from his wicked tongue exploded in a torrent of scorching sensations that left her weak, yet craving more.

Ewan crawled up the length of her body, pulling her thighs apart and putting one of her ankles on each of his shoulders. His cock jutted between them, glistening with a drop of moisture on the tip. Shona licked her lips, wanting to taste it. Wanting to fist his shaft in her hand and devour it like he'd done to her.

Her lover groaned. "Och, lass, dinna look at me like that. I want this to last and with the hunger written so plainly on your face, I'm likely to spend right here, right now."

Shona met his gaze, the both of them breathing hard and a sheen of sweat gleaming on their skin. All of the sudden, she was overcome with emotion, not just fueled by her desire for pleasure, but her wish to spend the rest of her days with this man. "I love ye."

"I love ye, too." Ewan leaned down, stretching her legs as he went and kissed her. The head of his shaft pushed into her opening as he did so, and she gasped.

Her breasts crushed against his chest, nipples aching and then he thrust home, burying himself to the hilt inside her. Their mingled groans were far-off to the hammering of her heart in her ears. He crushed his lips to hers in a sizzling, demanding kiss that sent spirals of ecstasy tunneling through her. When she thought she'd never catch her breath, his lips seared a path over her chin to her neck and then lower, until he captured a nipple between his teeth and suckled. Hard.

Slowly Ewan withdrew, lifting his head, he pressed his lips back to hers, his tongue plundering her mouth as his cock slammed back inside. With her ankles on his shoulders, her pelvis was tilted in a way that made the head of his shaft hit her at a different erotic, earth-shattering angle. Shona's mouth fell open as he hammered inside her, every stroke sending a spark of intensely enjoyable sensation rocketing through her.

All the while she held tight to the belt, letting him completely own her. Moan after moan left her lips. Between licking, nipping, and sucking her nipples, he kissed her mouth.

"Your body is mine. *Ye* are mine."

Shona abandoned herself to the swirl of emotion colliding inside her, finally allowing herself to completely surrender to Ewan's masterful seduction.

"Aye, Ewan. I am yours, completely and always."

His forehead fell to hers, their eyes locked on one another as they found a tempo that bound their bodies together. Flames licked at her inner thighs, her sex, and no amount of aroused moisture could put out the blaze. In fact, every move only heightened her enjoyment. Each stroke was so potent with pleasure, it seemed as though she had a mini-climax with every thrust.

"Ye're exquisite," he groaned. "I canna hold back much longer."

"Please dinna! Oh, Ewan!" She gasped in sweet torment as waves of throbbing ecstasy rocked her to the core. Shona was no longer in control of her limbs, everything sang with sensation and shook with her release.

Ewan drove deep inside her, harder, faster, sweat trickling down from his temples and an erotic growl ripping from his throat. As his pace slowed, he kissed her tenderly, sucking on her lower lip. He fell to the side, and pulled her flush against him.

"Ye can let go of the belt now," he murmured, a satisfied smile on his face.

"I'm not sure I can," Shona said, stretching out her legs and smiling. She let go, and wrapped her arms around Ewan. "That was amazing."

"Saints, love, it was beautiful."

He lazily traced the soft lines of her body while kissing her tenderly.

"No luckier man could I be, for Fate brought ye to me."

Shona smiled, knowing that he was right—in so many more ways than what he meant.

Epilogue

Two weeks later…

SHONA eyed Ewan from across the room. The night before had been incredible. It seemed every night they spent together outshone the previous. Her happiness in marriage bubbled over into every aspect of her life.

A storm had raged all through their lovemaking, and the morning brought with it a beautiful clear sky. Rays of sunshine gleamed through the open windows of their bedchamber, warming the damp chill in the room, and giving way to all sorts of tawdry thoughts, wishes, and every one of them having to do with the brawny Highlander stretching himself awake in their shared bed.

The past two weeks in the castle had been amazing. Everyone had been so welcoming and she'd not had to worry about a single pointed finger or word of witchcraft. She'd not believed it before, but now she found herself trusting wholeheartedly that she could live a contented life here with the Grant clan and Ewan — her *husband*.

The fact that he was hers had still not fully sunk in, and she felt like she had to pinch herself every few minutes to see if it was real. But it *was* real and she was *still* here. She'd not yet told her husband about her traveling through time, and she wasn't quite sure when a good time would be. She did want to tell him, but she needed to get her memories back first, else he think her a madwoman. Emma had promised to help. They planned to have their first *session*, as Emma called it, in just a few days' time.

Ewan was her husband, her soul mate, and he deserved the truth. Just not yet. She had to be able to tell him everything. And hopefully, in time, she could.

They were still enjoying an extended honeymoon as the MacDonalds had not yet come back to seek their vengeance, and she planned to enjoy every minute of it.

Ewan rolled up on one elbow and flashed her a wicked grin. "Morning, lass."

"Good morning, husband. How are ye feeling?" She still worried over all the injuries his body had worked to heal from — though after a few days, he'd not seemed to notice he was hurt at all. Somebody had to worry…

"I've not felt so good in days. Me thinks ye've the healing touch." He added a wink at the end, which sent Shona's body into a tailspin. Just that slight blink of one eye had a way of making her come undone.

She gulped as he stood, bare, save for the sprinkling of hair on his chest, legs, and the thatch that surrounded his proudly standing cock. Zounds, but her entire body now flamed, sparking erotic sensations between her thighs.

"I have your plaid," she blurted out, standing up and turning around to figure out where she'd neatly folded it after retrieving it from one of the clans' washerwomen.

Ewan grabbed hold of her arm and spun her around, pulling her flush against him. "I've no need for a plaid just yet."

Ewan grasped her chin, bent down and brushed his lips tenderly over hers. Too tenderly. A tease, he was. He pulled back, rubbing his thumb over her lower lip.

"Ye're so beautiful."

"Thank ye," she whispered, searching his eyes.

Love filled their depths making her belly warm. Ewan wrapped his arms around her, tucking her close. "Every time I look at ye, I am so overcome with love." He laughed. "I used to tease Logan about such. Used to tell him he'd been whipped into submission."

She couldn't hold back the smile of joy that touched her lips. "And now?"

"Och, now I know 'tis witchcraft."

Shona playfully tried to smack him, but he caught her arm in his grip and lifted her into the air, and then he kissed her soundly.

The End... for now...

Want to see what happens next in Shona and Ewan's story?
What happened to Rory?

Stay tuned for the next book in the series...
Highlander Undone

If you enjoyed **HIGHLANDER'S TOUCH**, *please spread the word by leaving a review on the site where you purchased your copy, or a reader site such as Goodreads or Shelfari! For more news on my books, sign up for my occasional newsletter at* www.elizaknight.com *I love to hear from readers too, so drop me a line at* authorelizaknight@gmail.com *OR visit me on Facebook:*
https://www.facebook.com/elizaknightauthor. *I'm also on Twitter:* @ElizaKnight *Many thanks!*

MORE BOOKS BY ELIZA

Have you read the first set of books in the Highland Bound series? Check out Eliza's erotic time-travel trilogy, **HIGHLAND BOUND**, that spurred the sequel, *Highlander's Touch*.

Book One: *Behind the Plaid*
Book Two: *Bared to the Laird*
Book Three: *Dark Side of the Laird*

Have you read the Stolen Bride series?

The Highlander's Reward
The Highlander's Conquest
The Highlander's Lady
The Highlander's Warrior Bride
The Highlander's Triumph
The Highlander's Sin
The Highlander's Charm (Kissing the Highlander
Anthology)
Wild Highland Mistletoe — *A Magnus and Arbella holiday*
novella
A Kilted Christmas Wish – a contemporary spin-off

Looking for a gripping Highland romance full of suspense, intrigue and love? Check out the HIGHLAND WARS series.

Highland Hunger
Highland Sacrifice
Highland Victory (Releasing 6/2015)

If you haven't read the other books, they are available at most e-tailers. Check out my website, for information on future releases www.elizaknight.com.

Eliza Knight

ABOUT THE AUTHOR

Eliza Knight is an award-winning, *USA Today* bestselling indie author of sizzling historical romance and erotic romance. While not reading, writing or researching for her latest book, she chases after her three children. In her spare time (if there is such a thing…) she likes daydreaming, wine-tasting, traveling, hiking, staring at the stars, watching movies, shopping and visiting with family and friends. She lives atop a small mountain, and enjoys cold winter nights when she can curl up in front of a roaring fire with her own knight in shining armor. Visit Eliza at www.elizaknight.com or her historical blog History Undressed: www.historyundressed.com

97618011R00150

Made in the USA
Columbia, SC
12 June 2018